SLIVER

..

Ira Levin's
NOVELS and *Plays*

SLIVER

Cantorial

Deathtrap

THE BOYS FROM BRAZIL

Veronica's Room

THE STEPFORD WIVES

Break a Leg

THIS PERFECT DAY

Dr. Cook's Garden

ROSEMARY'S BABY

Drat! The Cat!

Critic's Choice

General Seeger

Interlock

No Time for Sergeants

A KISS BEFORE DYING

SLIVER

A NOVEL

IRA LEVIN

BANTAM BOOKS / NEW YORK / TORONTO / LONDON / SYDNEY / AUCKLAND

This is, as the title page states, a novel, which means that everything in it is fictional. The author is grateful to the following people for advice and information on various subjects: Paul Busman, Gloria Dougal, Peter L. Felcher, Herbert E. Kaplan, Adam Levin, Jed Levin, and Genevieve Young.

SLIVER

A Bantam Book / March 1991

Book design by Jaya Dayal

Library of Congress Cataloging-in-Publication Data

Levin, Ira.
Sliver : a novel / Ira Levin.
p. cm.
ISBN 0-553-07292-7
I. Title.
PS3523.E7993S57 1991
813'.54—dc20 90-46204
CIP

*Published simultaneously in
the United States and Canada*

Bantam Books are published by Bantam Books, a division of Bantam Doubleday Dell Publishing Group, Inc. Its trademark, consisting of the words "Bantam Books" and the portrayal of a rooster, is Registered in U.S. Patent and Trademark Office and in other countries. Marca Registrada. Bantam Books, 666 Fifth Avenue, New York, New York 10103.

*Printed in the United States
of America*

BVG 0 9 8 7 6 5 4 3 2 1

TO
Dorothy Olding

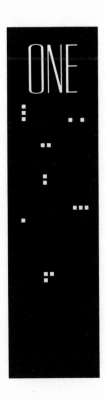

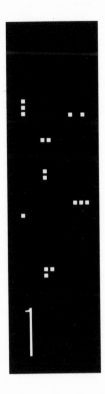

1

It was a good Monday morning to begin with—the Hoffmans slugging it out again, Dr. Palme on the phone with a suicidal ex-patient, the Coles' maid getting it off with one of their vibrators, Lesley and Phil meeting in the laundry room—and then it got even better. MacEvoy came into the lobby with a woman who looked like Thea Marshall, the same oval face, the same dark hair. Obviously she was there to look at 20B, repainted the week before.

He watched them ride up in the number-two elevator. She was beautifully built, tall and bosomy, in a good-looking medium-dark suit. Threw a glance his way then stood with a hand on her shoulder bag watching MacEvoy spieling about the central air conditioning and the Poggenpohl kitchen. Thirty-five or -six. A strong resemblance.

He put the 20B living room and bedroom on the masters and watched her come into the foyer and across the bare living room, her heels twanging on the parquet. She looked good from behind too as she went to the window and stood facing out over the lower buildings across Madison. "It *is* a glorious view," she said, and her voice, melodic and throaty, echoed Thea Marshall's.

He couldn't spot a wedding ring but she was probably married or living with someone. He was going to approve her no matter what, of course, assuming she decided she wanted the apartment. He crossed his fingers.

She turned from the window, looked around, smiled. Raised her face. Coming closer, she looked right at him—Thea Marshall looked right at him—knocking him breathless.

"WHAT A LOVELY light," she said. The shallow glass ceiling dish was sculpted in Art Deco curves. In its chrome center her small raspberry-clad reflection hung face down looking at her.

"Isn't it?" Mrs. MacEvoy said, coming up beside her. "They're all through the building. Truly, no expense was spared. It was planned as a condo originally. The rent is a bargain, considering."

The rent was high but not impossible. She walked back toward the foyer, turned, surveyed the room—freshly white-painted, twenty by twenty-two, the window wide and large, the floor parquet, a pass-through to the kitchen. . . . If the rest of the apartment was on a par, she would have to make a decision then and there, first shot out of the classifieds. Did she *really* want to leave Bank Street? Go through all the hassle of moving?

She went on to the foyer.

The kitchen was handsome—tan laminate, stainless steel. Fluorescent lighting under the cabinets, appliances trim and foursquare. Good counter space.

The bathroom beyond it was glitzy but fun. Black glass walls, black fixtures, chrome hardware; a large tub, a stall shower. Tube lights by the over-the-sink cabinet; another chrome-centered Art Deco dish in the black glass ceiling, smaller than the one in the living room.

The bedroom, at the end of the foyer, was almost as large as the living room, freshly white too, the left-hand wall all accordion-doored closets. Another wide window at the back, another great view—a slice of the yellowing park and part of the reservoir, the roof of a Gothic mansion on Fifth. More than enough space for the desk against the right-hand wall by the window, with the bed, of course, across from the window and facing it. She sighed at her upside-down self in the ceiling light, at Mrs. MacEvoy waiting in the corner by the door. "This is the first apartment I've looked at," she said.

Mrs. MacEvoy smiled. "It's a gem," she said. "I wouldn't let it slip through my fingers."

They went back into the foyer. Mrs. MacEvoy opened the linen closet.

She took another look around, thinking about her beautiful apartment on Bank Street with its high ceilings and working fireplace. And its rock club on the corner, its roaches, its two years of Jeff and six years of Alex.

"I'll take it," she said.

Mrs. MacEvoy smiled. "Let's go back to my office," she said. "You can fill out the application and I'll put it right in the works."

■   ■   ■

HE GOT ANTSY waiting for Edgar's call. It didn't come till late Wednesday afternoon. "Hello, Edgar," he said, killing both masters, "how are you?"

"Getting on tolerably well. You?"

"Fine," he said.

"The September statement is on its way; considering how the market's been behaving, I think you'll be pleased. About the building: I had Mills speak to Dmitri again about the lobby."

"Tell him to try it in Russian," he said. "That piece of marble is still there. I mean those two pieces."

"I'm sure the new piece is on order, I'll check and get back to you. And Mrs. MacEvoy has an applicant for twenty B. Did I tell you it was going vacant?"

"Yes," he said, "you did."

"Kay Norris. Thirty-nine, divorced. She's a senior editor at Diadem, the publishing house, so she ought to be nice and quiet. Credit history and references first-rate. Mrs. MacEvoy says she's good-looking. She has one cat."

"Is Kay her name or her initial?" he asked.

"Her name."

"Kay Norris."

"Yes."

Printing it on the clipboard, he said, "She sounds ideal. Tell Mills to see that everyone takes extra good care of her."

"I will. There's nothing else at the moment. . . ."

"Then don't let me keep you," he said. Hung up.

Underlined it: <u>KAY NORRIS</u>.

Older than he'd thought, thirty-nine.

Thea Marshall had been forty when she died; he drew a breath, sighed a long sigh.

He switched on the masters and put her living room on 1 and her bedroom on 2, the same as Monday morning. The bedroom glared, sunlight pouring through the bare window. He turned the brightness down. Up a little in the living room.

His hands on the console, he gazed at the two empty rooms

on the twin masters. The monitors spread away in multitiered wings, blue-white, flicking with movement here and there.

SHE CALLED ALEX on Thursday night and told him to come get his books.

"Oh God, Kay, I know I keep saying it but this is *really* the worst possible time, the semester starting. You'll have to keep them just a few more months."

"Sorry, I can't," she said. "I'm moving a week from tomorrow. Either pick them up or I'm putting them outside. I've lost my interest in medieval architecture. God knows why."

He hadn't heard about her breakup with Jeff. He sounded genuinely sorry. "It's *good* you're moving, it's a fine idea. Start fresh. What have you found?"

She told him about it. "And it's on the next-to-the-top floor," she said. "You can see some of the East River from the living room and a piece of Central Park from the bedroom. Daylight galore. It's a lovely neighborhood, lots of well-kept old buildings, low ones, and the Cooper-Hewitt Museum is a block away."

"Thirteen . . . Hundred . . . Madison . . ."—in the musing tone he used before putting her down. "A sliver building? Narrow site?"

She drew breath and said, "Yes . . ."

"Kay, that's where the man was decapitated in the elevator machinery last winter. Remember? The super? There've been three or four deaths there and it's only a few years old. I remember thinking it's a pity the address is Thirteen Hundred because it reinforces superstition. That was the lead-in they used on TV, 'Thirteen hundred is an unlucky number on Madison Avenue' or some such. Of course you're—" "Alex," she said, "I knew about that. Do you think that *I'm* superstitious? Why did you expect me to mention it?"

"I was about to *say*, of course you're *not superstitious*, but I thought you would want to know anyway, if you didn't."

"The books, Alex," she said.

They agreed he would come pack them on Sunday afternoon and have them removed during the week. They said good-bye, she hung up.

Old Reliable. Negative, negative, negative.

It was awful about the super but the apartment was great nonetheless. She certainly wasn't going to let Alex and some tabloid-TV newscaster sour her on it. Three or four deaths over three years wasn't remarkable; two apartments on a floor meant forty altogether, with couples, probably, in most of them— sixty or seventy people. Without counting the turnover. And the staff.

Felice rubbed against her ankle. She picked her up, cradled her on her shoulder, nuzzled purring calico fur. Said, "Ooh Felice, are *you* in for a surprise! A whole new world. No more roaches to play with. Poor you. At least I hope not. You never know."

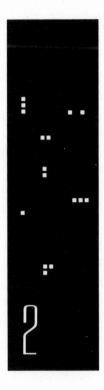

2

A man in a light blue sweater hurried ahead of her, straight-armed the thick glass door, and leaning, braced it open for her. She was carrying two flat cartons of precious breakables, one atop the other, and the doorman was getting someone with suitcases into the cab she'd gotten out of, so she was grateful. She smiled and thanked the man as she passed his arm. He was young and blue-eyed, good-looking.

A kneeling workman chip-chipped at the marble floor by the entrance to the mailroom. Above the elevator doors, B and 15 glowed in red digits.

The young man had crossed the lobby after her and was standing a few feet away on her right. She side-glanced at him as he looked from one indicator to the other, an I-Heart-New-York bag of groceries hanging from his hand. Reeboks, jeans, the light blue pullover. He was trim and clean-cut, her height, with reddish-brown hair. Twenty-five, twenty-six. He turned and said, "I could take one of those. . . ."

"They're light," she said. "But thanks."

He smiled at her—a dynamite smile, wide, bracketed with dimples, his blue eyes vivid.

She smiled and looked at the indicators—B and 15.

"Somebody's holding them," the very young man said, and turned and went to the side of the lobby, where security monitors glowed screens-upward in a tan marble block banked with greenery. The doorman came in—Terry, husky in his gray uniform, ruddy-faced. She had given him a ten-dollar handshake the last time she was there. He looked sadly at her and said, "Sorry I couldn't get the door."

"No problem," she said.

"The guy on fifteen is holding the elevator again," the young man said.

Terry shook his head on his way to the monitors. "Them Hoffmans . . ." He bent and peered, jabbed a button. Jabbed it longer, turning toward her. "Dmitri is just now putting the pads up in the other car," he said.

"It'll be a while before they get here," she said. "They were stopping to eat."

He headed for the door. "I'll buzz you when I see 'em."

"Mother Truckers!" she called over the cartons.

A howling police car raced up the avenue flinging red and white light as Terry opened the door for a jogger in a hooded sweatsuit. "It's coming," the young man said, returning. "Are you moving in?"

"Yes," she said. "In twenty B."

"I'm in thirteen A," he said. "Pete Henderson."

"Hi," she said, smiling over the cartons. "Kay Norris." The

jogger was watching her, jogging in place a few yards away; as she glanced at him, he looked toward the chip-chipping and watched that. Rawboned cheeks and a sandy mustache, fortyish.

"Where are you moving *from*?" Pete Henderson asked.

"Bank Street," she said to him. "In the Village."

The elevator door slid sideward and a schnauzer shot out pawing marble, leashed back by a woman in a blue denim pantsuit, mirror sunglasses, and a white kerchief. The man behind her wore mirror sunglasses and a baseball cap, a bomber jacket, chinos. He caught up with the woman and they hooked fingers as they followed the schnauzer toward the door.

She carried the cartons into the tan leathery elevator and turned around. Pete Henderson touched the 20 and 13 buttons alight, glancing at her. She smiled. He nodded to the jogger, who nodded back, touched 9, faced the closing door. Dark blotches spined his gray sweatsuit.

She looked at the changing number above the door, at the videocamera perched in the corner. Frowned at it. They were useful, of course, surveillance cameras, reassuring even—yet disquieting, with their intimation of unseen watchers.

The door slid open. The ninth-floor hallway was the same as the twentieth and the others she'd seen—a tan Parsons table and a gilt-framed mirror against a black-and-white-checked wall, brown carpet. The hooded man went to the right, to the A apartment, as the elevator door slid closed.

"I know the neighborhood pretty well," Pete Henderson said, "so if you need any information about stores or anything . . ."

"How's the market across the street?" she asked.

"Fine," he said. "These are from there. There's a Sloan's over on Lexington that's cheaper." The door slid sideward.

"Good to know," she said as he went out into the thirteenth-floor hallway—black and white checks, brown carpet.

Turning, he put a hand across the door's edge and smiled his dynamite smile. "Welcome to the building," he said. "I hope you enjoy living here."

Smiling at him over the cartons, she said, "Thank you."

He smiled at her, holding the door open.

She said, "They're getting heavy. . . ."

"Oh God, I'm sorry!" His hand flew; the door slid sideward. "See you!" he said.

"See you," she said as the door slid closed.

She smiled.

Cute, Pete Henderson.

Twenty-seven, tops.

AFTER THE MOVERS had gone and she had put the trash down the chute on the stairway landing, she washed up, poured herself a diet soda, and gave the place an objective survey. In the mellowing late-afternoon light her mix of contemporary and Victorian furniture looked far less grungy than she had anticipated. With the worst pieces replaced—maybe by something Art Deco, tying in with the ceiling lights—and with the cartons gone, books shelved, paintings and curtains hung, with the light and the views and the post-Ice-Age kitchen and bathroom and the *blessed quiet*, the apartment was definitely going to be all-around-better than the old one. And memory-free! The only thing she would miss was the fireplace. Felice would miss it too; she had always come hurrying at the sound of the screen's chain. . . .

She phoned Roxie and offered to pick Felice up that evening, but Roxie was working and wanted to leave things as planned: she would bring her over the next afternoon and help with the unpacking. Maybe they'd have dinner, Fletcher was away. Felice was fine.

She touched base again with Sara and listened to messages, not many and none that couldn't wait till Monday for action. With forecasts promising an ideal Indian-summer weekend, the day had been quiet even for a Friday. She told Sara to go home.

She decided to pick up the groceries she needed before

starting to work on the cartons; unpacked the answering machine and connected it to the desk phone, checked it out and left it on. Found her maize sweater and pulled it on over her shirt; fluffed her hair, did a one-two with lipstick and blush in the bathroom mirror, tucked her wallet and keys in the pockets of her jeans.

A tall balding man in a business suit came into the elevator on seventeen. They nodded and he reached to the lighted L button, stayed his hand, stepped back. On eight a square-jawed woman in dark green came in—stocky, with black bangs and straight hair. She eyed Kay with a week's worth of mascara and silver-blue eyeshadow, turned and faced the door. Her handbag and high-heeled pumps were snakeskin; the suit looked pricey too. Perfume suffused the air—Giorgio, a major overdose.

In the lobby, she saw Dmitri standing over to the right, his fists on his hips, his shaggy head down. She went to him, following in the Giorgio wake of the woman in green, who went into the mail room.

Dmitri raised his head; she thanked him for helping the move-in go smoothly. She had shaken his hand the other day at double the doormen's rate.

"Glad," he said, smiling, apple-cheeked. "I hope all is how you like, Meese Norris."

"It is," she said. Looked down at the new span of marble. "That looks good."

He shook his head. "No," he said. "Manager will say is too light. See? All around not-so-light, here *too* light. Will say is no good." He heaved a sigh.

"It's awfully close," she said.

"You think?" His dark eyes looked at her.

"It gets my vote," she said. "Thanks again."

"Glad, Meese Norris," he said. "Please. Any problem, you call."

She went to the door and pulled it open. The tall man who had been in the elevator waited under the rim of the canopy while the doorman, one she hadn't seen before, blew his whistle and waved at the traffic coming up the avenue. She held the door open behind her for a gray-haired man in a Beethoven sweatshirt; he caught the door's edge, looking at her with dark-ringed eyes. Smiling, she turned and went to the corner, Ninety-second and Madison.

Don't Walk changed to *Walk* as she joined the people waiting. She crossed Madison and strolled back up on the other side, looking into a restaurant, Sarabeth's; a hotel entrance, the Wales; another restaurant, Island, its front open to the mild weather. She went into Patrick Murphy's Market.

In narrow aisles stacked almost to the ceiling, she tracked down cat food and litter, yogurt and juices, cleaning supplies. The prices were higher than in the Village but she'd expected that. Her forties, she had decided, were going to be a decade of self-indulgence. She backtracked to the ice-cream case and took a chocolate chip.

When she pushed her cart onto the shorter of the two checkout lines, the man in the Beethoven sweatshirt came along after her with a basket. He was in his sixties, his mane of gray hair unkempt. Beethoven was gray too, hair and face, white lines washed thin on the purplish sweatshirt. The basket held a pack of Ivory and some cans of sardines. "Hi," he said, the slow shopper. Though maybe he'd gone somewhere else first.

"Hi," she said. "Why don't you go ahead of me?"

"Thanks," he said, and went around her as she drew back her cart. He turned before it and looked at her, a bit shorter than she, light glinting in his dark-ringed eyes. "You moved in today, didn't you," he said. His voice had a rasp in it.

She nodded.

"I'm Sam Yale," he said. "Welcome to Thirteen Hundred. A really rotten year."

She smiled. "Kay Norris," she said, trying to remember where she'd heard the name Sam Yale before. Or seen it?

"You brought a painting in the other day," he said, backing into space by the end of the counter. "Is that by any chance a Hopper?"

"Don't I wish," she said, following him with the cart. "It's by an artist named Zwick who admires Hopper."

"It looks good," he said. "At least from a third-floor window. I'm in three B."

"Are you an artist?" she asked.

"Don't I wish," he said, turning. He moved over and put his basket on the counter before the clerk.

She turned the cart against the end of the counter and unloaded it while Sam Yale—where had she seen that name?—paid for his soap and sardines.

He waited by the exit door with his I-Heart-New-York bag, watching her, while the clerk tallied her items, made change, bagged everything, two bags.

Streetlights shone under a violet sky when they came out. Traffic was jammed and honking, the sidewalk crowded. He said, "I figure that a woman who hires Mother Truckers wants to carry her own bags, am I right?"

She smiled and said, "At the moment."

"Fine with me. . . ."

Walking toward the corner, she looked beyond him at 1300's towering tan slab. Violet sky filled the two lanes of windows climbing its narrow front. She spotted her own window all the way up, one from the top on the right. "It's a goddamn eyesore, isn't it?" Sam Yale rasped.

She said, "The neighbors must have been thrilled."

"They fought it, for years."

She looked at him in profile. His nose had been battered long ago, his stubbly cheek was scarred. They were at the corner waiting. She said, "I've seen your name somewhere, or heard it."

"Son of a gun," he said, looking across toward the sign. "Long ago maybe. I directed. TV, in the 'golden age.' When it was black and white and live from New York." He glanced at her. "You were watching from your playpen."

"I wasn't allowed to watch," she said, "not till I was sixteen. Both my parents teach English."

"You didn't miss much," he said. "*Kukla, Fran, and Ollie;* the rest is overrated. Which isn't to say it wasn't better than today's crapola."

The sign changed. They started across the avenue.

"Now I remember," she said, smiling at him. "You directed a play Thea Marshall was in."

He stopped, dark-ringed eyes looking at her.

She stopped. "I saw a kinescope at the Museum of Broadcasting," she said. "Last year. I've been told a few times that I look like her." People hurried past them. "Let's not get killed," she said.

They walked on across the avenue.

"It's a strong resemblance," he said. "Even the vocal quality."

"I don't see it at all," she said. "Well, maybe a little . . ." She stopped on the sidewalk, faced him. "That's why you followed me," she said.

He nodded, his gray hair lifted by a breeze. "Don't worry, I'm not going to pester you," he said. "I just wanted a better look. She wasn't the love of my life or anything. She was someone I worked with a few times."

They walked toward the canopy.

"What did she die of?" she asked.

"A broken neck," he said. "She fell down a flight of stairs."

She sighed and shook her head.

The doorman hurried toward them—tall and thin, middle-aged, in glasses. "Hi, Walt," Sam Yale said.

Walt took her bags as she introduced herself.

"I have to get something in Feldman's," Sam Yale said. "Which play did you see?"

"It was set in a beach house," she said. "Paul Newman was in it, about *twenty-two*."

"*The Chambered Nautilus.*"

"Yes."

He nodded. "*The Steel Hour*, Tad Mosel. She wasn't bad in that."

"She was excellent," she said. "Everyone was. It was a moving play, beautifully done."

"Thanks," he said. Smiled at her. "See you," he said, and turned and went.

"See you," she said, and watched him go toward the house-wares store farther up the block, walking briskly—black sneakers, jeans, the faded purplish sweatshirt. She turned. Walt stood inside the lobby in his gray uniform, his back against the open door, looking at her, holding her two bags of groceries one-handed at his side.

"Sorry," she said. She went past him into the lobby and across it toward the open left-hand elevator, unsnapping her wallet as she went.

He brought the bags in after her and set them down on the floor by the door.

"Thanks," she said, smiling, offering her hand.

He stood up tall, his face lined, his steel-rimmed glasses blank with reflected light. He took her hand. "Thank you, Miss Norris," he said in a baritone surprisingly deep and resonant for his thin frame. "It's nice to have you in the building." He withdrew his hand and stepped back.

"Thanks, Walt, it's nice to be here," she said, and touched the 20 button alight.

The door slid closed.

She watched the changing number above it.

Sam Yale . . . Interesting. And amusing.

Sixty-five at least.

SHE CALLED THE folks and Bob and Cass, to tell them she was in and how great it was. Ate a strawberry yogurt gazing at glittering high-rises nearer the river, Matchbox traffic down below. She'd opened the window a few inches at either side; the traffic sounds were a pleasant urban hum compared to the grinding and growling outside the old apartment's second-floor windows.

She washed up, fed the portable player the first cassette of John Gielgud reading *Dombey and Son*, and—feeling uneasy, she wasn't sure why—went to work on the bedroom cartons.

EVEN WITH KAY NORRIS of the copper-brown eyes—a far nicer color than the green he'd expected—even with Kay Norris of the cream skin and the sable hair, *even with Kay Norris of the bosomed shirt and the buttocked jeans*, hanging up dresses and putting things into drawers got boring after a while. John Gielgud reading *Dombey and Son* didn't help.

He kept her on 2, switched the sound to 1, and scanned the monitors, swiveling in the chair, sipping the celebratory gin and tonic.

Half of them were out, either for the evening or the whole damn Indian-summer weekend. Half of the ones who were in were in their kitchens or watching the tube or reading.

He watched the Gruens arguing about their bridge signals, Daisy against using them, Glenn insisting. Frank and his fiancée coming to play.

He watched Ruby taking Polaroids of Ginger.

Mark coming in with flowers—a sound move but a night too late.

He watched the week's man from Yoshiwara setting the low dark table for two. Kay was arranging shoes on the closet floor. Both crouching in their different cultures. Nice bit.

He listened to Stefan and a fireman in Cincinnati who had answered the ad. Liz giving her mother the week's dirt from Price Waterhouse.

Bonanza! Dr. Palme came into the lobby, nodded to John as he went to the elevators. On a Friday evening? Of an Indian-summer weekend? Somebody had to be in desperate trouble.

Nina? Hugh? Michelle? Or could the good doctor be up to hanky-panky?

Kay was still doing shoes. He put Dr. Palme's office on 1, turned the sound higher, got up. Stretched—a good groaner, punching the small of his back—and brought the empty glass to the kitchen, went on into the bathroom.

Stood thinking about her, recalling her colors. . . .

Zipped. Flushed the black bowl.

He went into the kitchen and made another gin and tonic, lighter this time, hearing the creaks of Dr. Palme's leather chair, the ping and click of the fresh tape being put into the recorder. Stirring the drink with a fork handle, he looked out through the pass-through. She stood by the night table, a white phone at her cheek. He threw the fork on the dishes in the sink and hurried back in, switching the sound to 2 and the phone link on as he sat down in the warm chair. "—FOR THE MOON, DAMN IT," a man boomed—he turned the sound lower—"just a few minutes somewhere talking face to face! Is that such a big fucking deal?"

THE CLOCK SAID 9:53 when she hung up. She rolled onto her back, drew a deep breath and blew it out slowly, blinked a few times. Lay with an arm across her forehead, looking at her miniature self hovering beyond the foot of the bed in the center of the ceiling light.

Good for you, Tiny.

Over and done with. Finally. Forever.

She lay there a while longer, then reached to the night table and gathered the damp tissues. Got up and went into the bathroom, blowing her nose. Tossed the tissues into the black bowl and flushed it; moved to the black sink, patted cold water on her eyes and face. Took up the soap and scrubbed.

Looked at herself in the mirror as she toweled.

Good for you too.

And enough work for the day.

She called Roxie and got the machine. "Don't bother," she said, "I'll tell you tomorrow. I'm turning in."

She replaced Dickens and Gielgud with Segovia's guitar. Made the bed with stiff new clean-smelling linens, the yellow-flowered set.

She went into the kitchen, took a taste of the chocolate chip. Yum. Got the cleanser and sponge from under the sink, went into the bathroom.

She scrubbed the large black tub, bending and stretching, sweeping it rim to rim with sponge-strokes of foam. Gripped the chrome Art Deco spout and muzzled its mouth with her fingers; sprayed the foam down the curving black walls, chased it into the chrome-rimmed drain.

She ran the water hot on her wrist and started the tub filling. Squeezed a jade loop of Vitabath into the water, watched foam grow and spread. Dimmed the ceiling light—beautiful, those lights—dimmed it to a pale glow on the black glass and porcelain.

She undressed in the bedroom, lights out, the blind up. The distant cliff of light was Central Park West. Lights twinkled in the park's darkness, except where part of the reservoir lay.

She opened the left-hand side of the window; tugged with both hands at the rim of the bronze-bound panel, slid it a foot or so in its stubborn knee-high track. A warm breeze brushed her bare skin; the weather forecasts had been right for a change.

Ahead and far below—fourteen floors, she had worked it out—the pinnacled Gothic roof of the Jewish Museum lay lit by the windows of the apartment house alongside.

She smiled down at the dollhouse mansion.

Heights didn't bother her. Her office at Diadem was on the forty-eighth floor, one wall of it glass from floor to ceiling.

■   ■   ■

ONCE AGAIN AND worse than ever he wanted to kick himself for not having changed the bathrooms to white. Or gray, which would have been best. He had thought about doing it when he bought the building but the black fixtures had already been ordered and the Colonel had sworn that the Takai Z/3, which had just come onto the market, could pick up newsprint by matchlight. And it would have been hard explaining to Edgar and company, who already thought he was bonkers, why he was giving up a twenty-thousand-dollar deposit to change the color of the bathrooms. So he had stayed with black, Barry Beck's idea of classy design.

Between the black and the dim light and the damn foam, he could have been watching *Dynasty*.

Just about . . .

He had the brightness at max, so no contrast at all—everything soaked in gray, worse than a kinny. She was beautiful though, lying with her head resting on the corner of the tub by the wall, copper-brown eyes closed, her feet coming out through the foam now and then in the opposite corner. Sometimes just her toes. You could tell by the foam's slow rolling that she was stroking herself underneath it—nothing heavy, just relaxing, easing herself after the long day moving and the shit Jeff had dumped on her.

She had looked over at him—at her reflection in the light, of course—twice. The first time she'd smiled and waved a little. Knocked him out of the chair. He'd waved back and said "Hi, Kay"—gin and tonic number three. The second time she'd swung her head slowly from side to side, gazing at him.

He had her on both masters and was taping Dr. Palme and Hugh, which was too painful and distracting for simultaneous viewing. Rocky was in Chicago overnight for his nephew's wedding, so he was able to focus on her completely.

No, not completely. He had to look around in Rocky's apartment later on. No more drinks after this one. Seriously. It was a golden opportunity; maybe he could find an appointment schedule and settle whether or not he was being paranoid.

Her hand came out of the foam and stroked her throat, massaging; stroked the side of her neck. The sloshing water sounded glassy, brilliant. Behind it, the ventilator hummed, the guitar plinked. Segovia?

She frowned. Still thinking about that bastard Jeff most likely. How could she have lived with him for *two years*? It boggled the mind, despite Babette and Lauren and the other women he'd seen put up with exactly the same kind of turd. Jesus, Kay. . .

He leaned back, swiveled, fished with a foot under the console. Hooked out the leather pig and pulled it closer; crossed his feet on its back, wiggled his bare toes. Drank from the glass, watching her. Held the glass in his lap, its wet base pressed in his hair.

He had undressed when she did.

He sucked a sliver of ice, watching her. The two of her, side by side on the masters.

Beautiful . . .

. . . the quick-fingered guitar, the pine scent, the hissing foam . . . the hot silky water, herself so smooth in it . . .

But something was bugging her. . . .

A sense of a missed signal. Of odd vibes that had come at her that day, *before* Jeff, vibes she'd been too rushed to pick up on . . .

From Sam Yale? When he'd stopped in the middle of the avenue and looked at her with those insomniac eyes? Had he been lying about his strictly professional relationship with Thea Marshall? In a Gothic or thriller he would have been. . . .

What was definitely odd about him was his living *there*, in 1300 Madison Avenue. Old directors in sweatshirts and jeans lived in rent-controlled apartments on the West Side, or down in the Village or SoHo, among the actors and artists and writers. What was he doing in a new high-rise on the Yupper East Side? When had he stopped directing? Why?

What did Pete Henderson do, shopping for groceries on a Friday morning?

Worked nights, worked at home, was on vacation, had won the lottery. Whichever it was, what a doll—the dynamite smile, the vivid blue eyes, the reddish-brown hair. Nothing odd about *his* vibes; he was young and smitten, like assistant editors. If he were fifteen years older . . . Or ten . . .

The jogger in his hooded sweatsuit, jogging in place, watching her—was he the one who was bugging her? He'd been attractive in the glimpse she'd gotten, the rawboned cheeks and sandy mustache. Marlboro Country. Married or gay, be sure.

Walt, when she'd tipped him? His light-blanked eyes . . .

The blond mover? No missing *her* signals . . .

She shifted under the foam.

Maybe what was really bugging her was being alone. . . . No Felice, no nobody, on the first night in a new apartment. Strangers above and strangers below, a stranger next door. (*V. Travisano*, the 20A doorbell said. Victor? Victoria?)

She sat up and leaned back, her arms along the end and side of the tub. Looked at the glowing ceiling light, the curved pale patch in its dark iris, the tiny figure seated in it.

She blew foam from her breasts—left, right, chilling her hard nipples. Peered at the tiny dark-haired figure . . .

Lifted her leg from the water, watching the tiny leg, foam sliding from her heel . . . Arched her foot . . . watching . . .

Touched her toe to the tip of the chrome Art Deco spout . . .

Slid low in the water, foam islands breaking . . .

Maybe what she really needed . . . maybe? . . . was an easing of the tension. . . .

HE TIMED IT so they came together.

It was great.

For what it was . . .

Sprawled with one foot on the pig and one on the floor, he caught his breath, his hand full of tissues and himself.

He stayed for a while without moving, just breathing, watching her doing the same in the foam-flecked water. Both of her, turned toward the wall, showing their Thea Marshall profiles, eyes closed. So doubly beautiful . . .

He must never put himself in her path again.

He knew. He wasn't planning to . . .

If it happened, all right, but it was to be AVOIDED.

He *knew.*

Remember Naomi.

He did. And felt rotten about her, still.

He got up, holding himself with the tissues. Kay was back in business too, the two of her, sitting up, soaping their underarms.

He went into the bathroom. Dropped the tissues into the black bowl, flushed it. Shook his head, sighing.

It was going to be hard just watching her . . .

Now that he'd seen her live and in color. . . .

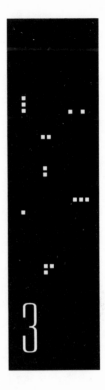

3

Walled with dark-grained wood and curtained with tiers of chain rippling up toward its three-floors-high ceiling, the Grill Room of the Four Seasons is where editors and publishers, those who haven't moved downtown, lunch with one another and their or someone else's cherished writers. At midday on that spacious stage (hung upstage right with a cloud of brass rods), dark-suited men and varicolored women settle in twos and fours at the good and the less good tables, on the good and the less good levels, like the birds convening on Hitchcock's jungle gym. They peck at who's with whom and who looks how, who's moving where, who's buying what. Bobbing waiters bring them food, artfully arranged, in portions far too large for birds.

Seating herself on a banquette on the good level, at a less good table, Kay saw, up on the less good level, a rawboned cheek and a sandy mustache. The man seated in profile looked like the jogger in 9A, but she'd only glimpsed him once, nearly a week before, and some thirty feet separated them. He was with a white-haired man, an editor whose name and current house escaped her.

Her bearded guest Jack Mulligan had written, under a pen name, sixteen romantic thrillers; she had edited the last four, best sellers. He overwrote—jungles of entwined and floriferous prose; she cut paths through branching metaphors, chopped away vines of adverbial clauses, changed profusions of viridescent foliation into masses of green leaves. He had followed her from Random to Putnam to Diadem. Publishing is played like checkers.

Lately he had become a media celebrity; people stopped at the table to congratulate him and shake his hand. "Right on, Jack!" they said, and, "It's about time someone got even!"

"No, no, really," he said, beaming. A month or so earlier, he had claimed and then denied responsibility for a computer virus, ultimately untraceable, that had laid low a noted journal, stripping its data banks of all names and words containing the letters F and Y. The journal's review of his *Vanessa's Lover*, though a quote-studded rave, had thoughtlessly given away one of the book's surprises. He had faxed four pages of fury at the editor; the customary short whine from a reader had been published.

When the journal howled with its wound, Mulligan's friends had believed his swear-you-won't-tell phone calls. He had three sons in computers, pioneer hackers grown and working in artificial intelligence and security-systems design; and furthermore, at about the same time the journal lost its F and Y words, the author of the careless review had vanished from the memories of more than half the commercial computers that till then had known and trusted him. To representatives of the District Attorney's office and the FBI, however, Mulligan had said—flanked by Paul, Weiss, Rifkind, and others—no, no, he'd spoken in jest, he'd said he *wished* he had done it, he deplored vandalism, and so on and so forth. His twinkling eye had subsequently appeared on *Live at Five*, *A Current Affair*, and *Nightline*'s panel on computer insecurity.

The upshot of the matter, as the journal and the reviewer struggled to reorder their lives, was exactly what one would expect: booming sales for *Vanessa's Lover* and a request from Mulligan's agent for a cosmic advance for a two-paragraph outline of *Marguerite's Stepfather*. It was in the faint hope of reducing that request that Kay, with her chief's wholehearted endorsement, was lunching Mulligan at the Seasons.

"Do you know the white-haired man on the mezzanine?" she asked when they were finally left to themselves. "He used to be with Essandess; I can't remember his name or where he is now."

Jack scratched ,his ear, turned, scanned the walls and the ceiling, turned to her. "That's the same table where Bill Eisenbud had his heart attack," he said. "Wasn't he a dear man? What a shame. We had a house next to them on the Vineyard the summer of 'seventy-three. No, 'seventy-four. A lovely house with a big screened-in porch. All incastellated with wisteria vines."

She said, "Do you know him?"

"No, it was 'seventy-*three*," he said. " 'Seventy-four was South America." He shook his head. "No," he said. "I wonder if Sheer is writing another book. He said he wasn't. He's odd about money. We shared a cab afterwards and I gave him a five when I got out—there was a little under seven on the meter—and he insisted on calculating my exact change to the nickel."

The waiter came, bobbed for their drink order, left.

" 'Sheer'?" she said. "You know the man with him?"

He looked at her across the table. "I thought you watched *Nightline*," he said.

"I *did*," she said.

"On what? That antique portable? Do you mean to say that's still the only set you own?"

"He was on it too?"

"The doom-and-gloom man," Jack said. "The one who wrote the book about computers making us vulnerable to all kinds of disasters. Like getting paid back for spoiling a story."

She said, "Hubert Sheer . . . Of course, I remember now. He was hostile to you. . . ."

Jack chuckled. "Wasn't he though," he said. "But perfectly nice in the cab. He apologized sincerely for that 'juvenile mentality' crack. They dragooned him for the show at the last minute, somebody canceled. He doesn't like doing TV, though Koppel certainly had a hard time cutting him off once he got started. He wrote the book years ago."

"I think he lives in my new building," she said.

"Oh, does he? Yes, he could, he was going on up Madison. . . ."

They looked at the menus.

She glanced up and he was watching her, Hubert Sheer. Sat smiling, his cheeks and forehead flushed, his thinning hair sandy like his mustache.

She gave him a low-scale smile and nod.

He nodded, redder.

The waiter put down her Perrier and lime, Jack's Glenlivet.

They ordered—veal paillards, grilled salmon.

Jack offered his glass. "To *Marguerite's Stepfather*."

She touched hers to it. "To Diadem's solvency."

"Party pooper."

They talked about a new best seller—good but not *that* good—the Washington scandal, the unpromising Broadway season.

The white-haired man came grinning; a few yards behind him, Hubert Sheer limped against a cane. "Kay!" the man said. "Martin Sugarman. How are you?"

"Martin!" she said. "How nice to see you!"

He bent and kissed her cheek. "You look wonderful!"

"So do you!" she said. "Jack Mulligan, Martin Sugarman."

"A real pleasure!" Sugarman said, holding Jack's hand in both of his, pumping. "It's about time someone got even!"

"No, no, really," Jack said, beaming.

Hubert Sheer limped up, red-faced, in tan tweed, a brown shirt, rust tie. His eyes, gray under sandy brows, shone with suppressed excitement. He smiled at her, braced against his cane.

"Kay, this is Hubert Sheer, who's just signed to do a book with us. Kay Norris."

"Congratulations," she said, smiling, offering her hand.

He took it backhanded in his left, hot and moist. "Thank you," he said. "We're neighbors."

"I know," she said.

His gray eyes widened; he let go her hand, caught Jack's. "Hello," he said.

"Hello," Jack said. "What happened to you?"

"I fractured my ankle," Sheer said. "The day before yesterday." He smiled at her. "My bike fell apart when I was on my way to make copies of the outline. Do you think God is trying to tell me something?"

"Maybe 'Break a leg,' " she said.

He smiled. Sugarman laughed.

"I thought you were through with books," Jack said.

"So did I," Sheer said to him, "but Marty called me the day after *Nightline* with an idea that really excited me." His gray eyes swung back to her, piercing. "Television," he said. "A complete overview of the way it's impacted on society so far and *will* impact in the years ahead. Every aspect of it, from soap operas to surveillance cameras to the effect camcorders are having on world affairs. I'm even planning to—" "Rocky . . ." Sugarman said.

Sheer looked at him, at her. Went redder, smiled.

"I won't breathe a word," she said, smiling.

"Please keep it under your hats," Sugarman said to her and Jack. "It's very early stages."

"It sounds fascinating," Jack said. "And right in line with your other book."

"Yes," Sheer said, "I'm really excited about it. I've been taking a crash course in Japanese. I'm going over there next week to visit factories and interview manufacturers and designers."

"It was kismet," Sugarman said. "I got the idea in the morning, and that night, there he was on *Nightline*, the perfect writer for it. Oh look, Joni's here." He touched Sheer's shoulder. "You go ahead, Rocky, I'll catch up with you downstairs."

Sheer looked at her. "Do you bike?" he asked.

"Yes," she said. "I don't have one. . . ."

"Neither do I," he said, smiling. "A bus got it. They rent them in the park, by the boathouse. Can I call when I get back?"

"Please do," she said, smiling. "I hope it's a productive trip."

"Thank you," he said, smiling, red-faced.

He said good-by to Jack, limped away.

Sugarman leaned closer. "Terrifically perceptive," he said. "Makes all kinds of surprising connections. Did you read *The Worm in the Apple*?"

"No," she said, "I'd like to."

"I'll messenger you a copy this afternoon," he said. "Incidentally, he asked to be introduced, if that's of any interest. He's forty-three, divorced, and an exceptionally nice guy. Well, I'd have come over and said hello anyway. Wonderful seeing you, and meeting *you*, Jack. Congratulations. In all departments!" He turned and went toward the better tables.

She smiled after him, waved at Joni waving at her.

" 'Rocky'?" Jack said, cutting his veal.

"It beats Hubert," she said.

She turned and looked over her shoulder, through gold-threaded glass, at Sheer's tan back beyond the rim of the wide stairway, going down slowly, close against the left-hand railing.

Going down out of sight, slice by slice.

■   ■   ■

SHE BROUGHT THE window measurements in to Bloomingdale's custom drapery department and ordered white silk for the
living room and green-and-white-striped chintz for the bedroom.
On the way to contemporary furniture she spotted a high-style
scratching post—brown cork doughnuts on a giant chrome sta-
ple. Only at Bloomie's . . .

She worked out at the Vertical Club, sweating as she battled
the biceps machine, the leg press, the stomach board. Pedaled
an exercise bike awhile.

Came out of the elevator to Felice's meowing and the hallway
full of fat pink leather suitcases, a herd of them, blocking her
door and butting open the door of 20A, where across the foyer,
in her own kitchen flipped over, a young woman in a white coat
said into the phone, "No! I meant exactly what I said!" Seeing
Kay, she raised a spread hand, every finger ringed. Mimed a
groan, looked to heaven, to Kay, shrugged piteously. She was
model-gorgeous, slim, in her early twenties, with a cap of
straight blond hair. The belted white coat was the one that had
been on *Elle*. "Fuck both of you!" she said in a furry voice, and
slammed the phone to the wall. "I'll get those right out of your
way," she said, coming to the door. She opened it wider, kneed
a suitcase to hold it. "I'm sorry, your poor cat's going crazy. I
guess he never smelled India before." She corraled pink suitcases. "When did you move in?" she asked.

"A week ago . . ." Kay said, sidestepping past the stairway
door.

"Let him out," V. Travisano said, flashing a smile at her.
"Give him a treat. I'm a cat person too."

"She's a she." She put down her briefcase and the Bloomingdale's bag, shifted a suitcase, unlocked the door.

Felice raced out and prowled a lightning cloverleaf where
leather met carpet, sniffing, sniffing, sniffing, sniffing.

"Oh, she's a beauty! I love calicoes. What's her name?"
"Felice."
"That's a nice one. 'Felice . . . .' Mine is Vida Travisano."
"That's a nice one too."

She laughed. "Thanks," she said, "I made it up myself."

"Mine's Kay Norris."

"That's nice."

"My parents made it up." She picked up straining India-crazed Felice.

Vida Travisano hauled in the last suitcase. "You're a big improvement over the poor Kestenbaums," she said. Smiled in the doorway in her *Elle* white coat, a glittering hand on the jamb, white boots crossed at the ankles. "Did you hear about the Kestenbaums?" she asked.

"Felice! Stop it! No," Kay said. "No. I didn't. . . ."

"They were an interesting kind of couple," Vida Travisano said. "He was American and she was Korean. Very beautiful; she could have been a model. They never mentioned what they did. Entertained a lot. Then he developed MS—multiple sclerosis?—and just started *melting*. And she's pushing him in and out in the wheelchair. . . . And I mean, your heart *breaks*, but it's so *depressing*. . . . You know? They moved out to this place in California where they're doing advanced research on it. It looked like they wouldn't be able to, she was crying about it a few months ago; it costs a fortune and their insurance didn't cover it. Thank God they got the money from someplace. If you want to dish sometime, ring the bell. I'm going to be around till November ninth, then it's—" The phone rang. "Oh, *shit*. Then it's off to sunny Portugal. See you." Backing inside, she waved at Felice. " 'Bye, Felice!" She closed the door as the phone rang.

Felice hit the carpet sniffing suitcase prints, berserk.

Dmitri came and put up the bookshelf supports in the living room, drilled the X's she had marked low on the kitchen wall. She put the scratching post up and showed Felice what it was, rubbing her front paws against the cork doughnuts. Lots of luck.

She hung Roxie's falcon in the foyer; both it and the Zwick looked better apart. She put books on the shelves while Claire Bloom read *To the Lighthouse*. Introduced herself at the Corner Bookstore on Ninety-third Street—it never hurts to get window space.

She called the folks and thanked them for the bowl, which had Art Deco lines and would look fine on the new coffee table when it came. Got into the usual argument with Dad when he told her to tell Bob to call.

She read the trade paperback edition of Hubert Sheer's *The Worm in the Apple,* the first four chapters. Called Roxie. "And it's terrific so far, he's a *very good writer.*"

"So what's the story?"

"There is no story," she said, lying on the bed playing with Felice's white ear. "We have a *sort* of a date to go biking after he's back from a trip. I don't even know how long he's going to be gone. Japan. He's leaving this week sometime."

"It sounds kind of vague."

"It is," she said, watching Tiny and her teeny cat in the ceiling light. "I told you, there's no story. But he's awfully attractive and the book is great. What's doing with you and Fletcher?"

She held winter dresses against herself in the bedroom mirror. Wasn't thrilled.

Put books on the end of the top shelf, standing on the stepladder, reaching.

Felice, in the kitchen, stood watching the base of the below-the-sink cabinet.

WHO WOULD EVER think, with all the restaurants in the city, *thousands* of them, that she and what's-his-name, Rocky's editor, would zero in on the same one for lunch? Incredible . . . Unless the Four Seasons had turned into some kind of hangout for writers and editors since he'd been there . . . But it still had class; the Steins were taking Lesley's parents there for their silver anniversary, Vida and Lauren suggested it to johns. No, it was just another of life's amazing coincidences. . . .

It was a shame she liked Rocky. They'd be a good match, when you considered how much they had in common. . . .

He couldn't let it make any difference though.

Not when Rocky had an appointment at eight A.M. Osaka time a week from Tuesday in the Takai Company's showroom, and they'd probably made an extra light or two for display purposes or at least had some eight-by-ten glossies in the album. Wouldn't any manufacturer, let alone a smart hot-for-more-business Jap?

Stay cool. Think. No time for panic. It's Sunday night, no, Monday morning; Rocky's flight leaves JFK Friday morning at eleven.

Think.

Maybe the bike wasn't really a total washout. . . . Look at the positive side. It had left Rocky with his foot in a cast, limping around 9A with a cane. . . .

SHE USUALLY WORKED at home one day a week—Tuesday or Wednesday, depending on her appointments and whatever meetings were scheduled—and got as much done, with minimal phone calls from Sara, as in two days at the office. She worked most evenings too, and three or four hours on weekends; read manuscripts in bed from six to eight each morning.

Her at-home day that week was Tuesday, the 24th of October, a day that at its end was declared by all the weathermen on all the channels to have been the most glorious day of that glorious season. Their stats were backed by footage of turquoise skies, fiery trees, and upturned faces—footage shot for the most part in Central Park.

To sit that glorious morning with a slice of fiery park and turquoise reservoir beyond one's left shoulder and to be *editing a book*, even a fine book such as the one she was glad to be working on, was—work. Especially for a country girl . . .

She turned, lifting her glasses; looked out at a skein of geese flying down to the turquoise; leaned to watch the geese merge with geese flying up from beneath, feathering water between them.

She lowered her glasses, turned and read.

Made marks.

Drew in breath as papers stirred by the window, inches open. . . .

She hung on till the end of the part.

Gathered Adidas, jeans, the burgundy turtleneck, the Irish wool sweater. Felice, meatloafed in the middle of the bed, watched her.

When she was more than halfway around the dirt track skirting the lake of chain-link-fenced reservoir, striding along behind her sunglasses high on the turquoise sky, fiery trees, edged air, motley people, bold squirrels (should've brought peanuts), and soaring fowl, feeling better than she had in over two years and maybe in seven or eight, she rounded a leftward curve and saw on the track ahead Sam Yale coming toward her among the pay-no-attention-to-the-arrows crowd, looking as high on the glorious morning as she was, walking with his arms swinging and gray hair blowing, beaming at the water on his right. She slowed as he came nearer, squinting upward. "Sam!" she called. He stopped and raccoon-eyed her; a jogger swerved past him.

She moved onto the shoulder of the track, lifting her glasses. "Kay," she said. "Norris."

He smiled. "Hi!" he said. Stood smiling while three men walked past him, flat-footed, bare-limbed, elbows pumping.

She took the glasses off as he came across and onto the shoulder with her, in jeans and black sneakers, a gray windbreaker zipped to the collar of a red flannel shirt. "What a day!" he said, rubbing his hands.

"Sensational, isn't it?" she said.

"And how."

"I don't want to stop. Come on, walk with the arrows, it won't hurt you."

"Arrows?" he said, following her onto the track.

"On the base of the fence," she said, putting the glasses on. "Every once in a while."

"Hey, slow down," he said, behind her on her left, "I'm out here for pleasure."

She slowed down. Smiled at him as he caught up and strode along. His battered face wasn't bad-looking for sixty-six. In the stamp-sized picture in *Television's Golden Age* he'd been a soulful wunderkind with wavy dark hair, his eyes dark-ringed even back then.

He smiled at her. "Did the book business declare a holiday?" he asked in his raspy voice.

"I work at home sometimes," she said.

"Nice work," he said.

"I picked the wrong day," she said. "The right one, I mean. How do you know I'm in publishing?"

He dropped behind her for a stroller with a pacifier-gagged baby in it, pushed by a teenaged girl in a sheepskin jacket and a headband radio.

He moved up alongside her. "I passed the truck the day you moved in," he said. "Lots of cartons with the Diadem logo."

"Oh," she said.

"Great rolltop desk. How old is that?"

"Eighty, eighty-five years."

"What do you do?" he asked.

"I'm an editor," she said. "There, there's an arrow."

"Jesus," he said, "they painted that when *McKinley* was president. It's practically invisible. Nobody's expected to follow *those*."

"What do you *mean*?" she said as joggers bounded past them. "They're there. Who said you're not expected to follow them?"

"It's common knowledge," he said, dropping behind her for a pair of nuns. A horse cantered by on the bridle path to her right, cantered down a fiery arcade, a chestnut mare ridden by a man in a checked jacket, black boots, riding breeches.

Sam moved up on her left. "What a day," he said.

"A holiday for directors?"

"Every day, for retired ones. Will you look at that skyline?"

She looked at shining ranks of white and steel towers south of the park, the beveled Citicorp Building, the Empire State's needle against the turquoise. "Fantastic," she said.

"You're not in Kansas any more, Dorothy."

She gave him a sidelong look as they walked. "What had *Kansas* on it?" she asked.

He smiled at her. "Nothing," he said. "It's in your mouth."

"I don't have an accent," she said, bridling. "I worked to get rid of it."

"Excuse me," he said. "I'm psychic."

They detoured around a television crew pointing a peacock-logoed minicam up at fiery trees.

"You forget," he said when they were back on the left-curving track, "I directed. The ear is tuned." He tapped it with a fingertip. "To the average person, no, you don't have an accent. Except on words like 'hello' and 'how are you.' "

"I *don't*," she said.

"Very slight," he said, smiling. "Really, very slight. Only an extremely gifted pro would catch it." He dropped behind her for a wheelbarrow full of dark cinders pushed by a brown-uniformed man.

He moved up alongside her. She said, "I looked you up in a book we published a few years ago, *Television's Golden Age*."

"Wow, what a great title," he said. "Who thought of that? Not you I hope."

"It happens to be a very good title," she said. "It tells what the book is about in clear understandable English."

"I stand corrected," he said.

"No, it wasn't mine," she said.

They walked toward the gatehouse at the south end of the reservoir. Joggers bounded past them.

"So were you impressed?" he asked.

"Very," she said. "Puzzled too."

"Why it all ended? Easy. I'm a recovering alcoholic."

"I'm sorry," she said, looking at him. "Glad you're recovering though. That wasn't what I meant, although—I'm sorry, I shouldn't have brought this up. I'm sure you don't want to talk about it."

He said, "Initials T.M.?"

She sighed, nodded.

"Tom Mix. Always a favorite."

She smiled.

"You cross-checked our credits," he said.

"Yes," she said. "She was in almost twenty plays that you directed."

"They liked her at *Steel* and *Kraft*."

"You won two Directors Guild Awards and an Emmy," she said, "and your career stopped short the year she died."

"What do you edit?" he asked. "Kissing with castles in back?"

"I have," she said.

"One thing had nothing to do with the other," he said. "We hadn't seen each other for two or three years at that point. Our paths had separated, in every sense. I was out on the coast doing movies of the week. She was here doing soaps."

They crossed the terrace before the stone gatehouse, passing people at the fountains, people stretching themselves over legs braced on bench backs, a jostle of teenagers in red track suits, a man in red clapping at them.

"If you want the truth," Sam said, "she wasn't a very good actress."

"I noticed," she said.

"Or a very good person," he said. "She was vain and greedy. Totally self-centered. Spiteful. Inconsiderate. Petty. I was crazy about her."

"*Why?*" she asked.

"I said 'crazy,' " he said. "Who can explain it?" He looked at the track ahead, sighed. "Who can tell you why?" he said. "It was an enchanted morning. Across a crowded television studio . . ."

The teens in red track suits loped past them in ones and twos as they followed the curve to the east of the reservoir.

"Are you completely retired?" she asked.

He said, "I teach a little. Acting, directing . . ."

"How long have you been in the building?"

"Since it went up," he said. "Three years."

They walked on.

Joggers bounded past them.

A red-suited teen.

"If you're wondering what I'm doing up in this neck of the woods," he said, "I'm a charity case."

"No I wasn't, don't be silly," she said, "everybody lives all over the place nowadays, it's great, it's one of the best things about the city."

He said, "The Carnegie Hill Cultural Enrichment Foundation. Do I have to explain what their purpose in life is? One of the ways they think they'll achieve it is by seeding the neighborhood with hard-up artsy types. I get the apartment rent-free plus a stipend. And it's the ideal location for me." He smiled at her. "Smithers around the corner on Ninety-third. The Smithers Treatment Center. I was in it for a while when the building was under construction." He dropped behind her for a pair of joggers, a man and a boy, in sweatshirts stenciled BLIND and GUIDE.

They came to the esplanade at Ninetieth Street, went down the wide pebbled steps. A television crew stood in the bridle path, pointing a minicam at passers-by looking up at fiery trees.

"Oh great," she said, "we'll be on the six o'clock news. Tomorrow's joke at the office."

"I'm that bad?"

"You know what I mean."

"Don't panic," he said. "There's always a solution."

They walked past the eye-logoed minicam with his middle finger in the air.

They crossed the park drive and Fifth Avenue. Walked along Ninetieth Street past the iron-fenced garden behind the Cooper-Hewitt Museum. He said, "That was Andrew Carnegie's retirement home."

"I didn't know that," she said, looking at the brick-and-stone Palladian mansion.

"That's why we're on Carnegie Hill," he said. "This was farmland when he bought it. His steel company eventually became U.S. Steel; I did so many *Steel Hours* I feel I'm on home territory. This is the house Robert Chambers lived in."

"I know the name. . . ."

"The preppie who strangled the girl in the park."

"Oh."

"We're a mixed bunch up here."

They turned at the corner, headed up Madison.

"Television must have been very different early on," she said.

"And how," he said. "Everything going out live, no tape, no retakes. Every show an opening night—blown lines, missing props, but alive, electric, the actors going for broke. The scenery was painted different shades of gray, color didn't matter."

She said, "Why don't you write your memoirs? Or talk them into a tape recorder. It could be interesting."

"My 'memoirs'?" He smiled.

"Yes," she said. "Give it some thought. Do you know Hubert Sheer? He lives in our building, in nine A."

He shook his head.

"He's a writer," she said, "a good one. He's doing a book on television that he'd probably like to talk to you about. I'll have to introduce you. But think about doing something of your own. Really, it could be salable. If you want to go into serious personal material, fine. Or you could keep it light and amusing if you like, which I'm sure you could do. Whatever feels comfortable."

He smiled. "I'll think about it," he said. Gestured at Jackson
Hole as they passed it. "Want some coffee?"

"Can I have a rain check?" she asked. "I have to go to the bank
and get back to work."

They crossed Ninety-first Street. She took her sunglasses off.
"I'm glad we met," she said, offering her hand.

"Same here," he said, shaking it, smiling at her.

"Think about it," she said. "I'm not just making nice."

"Okay, I'll think," he said. Turned and went.

Came back. "Hey," he said. "I was kidding about the accent.
I saw the return address on a package of yours in the mailroom
the other day. Norrises in Wichita."

Smiling, she said, "Thanks for telling me."

"I wouldn't want you to think you wasted your time," he said.
"No accent at all, not a whisper." He smiled at her, turned and
went.

She turned, put the glasses on, waited for the sign to change.
Jigged on her toes, smiling up at the turquoise sky.

SHE PRESENTED THREE books at the pre-sales conference
Wednesday; the marketing people liked two and loathed the third
less than she and the rest of the editorial department had
expected. She spent an hour at Saks—bought a claret silk dress
and some underthings.

Had long talks that evening with Bob and with Meg Hunter,
who called from JFK between planes to London; they relived
Syracuse for over an hour. She shaved her legs while Claire
Bloom read the last part of *To the Lighthouse*, and Felice, on the
bathmat, licked and scrubbed.

She worked most of Thursday with a woman from Newark
whose first novel, witty science fiction, was two hundred pages
too long. Went to the Warner party for their Catherine the Great

bio, upstairs at the Tea Room—*everyone* there for champagne and blini and caviar.

Opened her cab door to white light and a caring-looking woman with a microphone. "Do you live here?" A man, "Did you know Hubert Sheer?" The woman, "Do you know this building is being called the Horror High-Rise?" Walt fended them off, ushering her toward the door. "He kicked me! Did you get him kicking me? Hey you! Doorman! You're in trouble, *shithead*!"

Walt looked out through the glass door as he closed it. "The scum of the earth," he said in his deep baritone. "It was like feeding time at the zoo before. You're lucky you're late."

She said, "Hubert Sheer?"

He turned toward her, looked at her through his glasses. Nodded. Glanced away and stepped back, pulling the door open. People went out. He closed the door.

"What happened?" she asked.

He drew a breath and took his glasses off. Looked at her with watery hazel eyes, his lined face pale. "He fell in the shower," he said. "He had a cast on his foot, and a plastic bag taped around it to keep it dry—and he slipped and hit his head."

"He's *dead*?" she said.

He nodded, opened the door. A man came in saying, "Jesus Christ . . ." Walt closed the door, watching her. Said, "Did you know him, Miss Norris?"

She nodded.

"Would you like to sit down?"

She couldn't decide.

He showed her to a bench by the block where the monitors were, took her briefcase as she sat. He put his glasses on, held the briefcase with both hands. Bent to her over it. "Someone from his agent's office came to check," he said. "He wasn't returning his phone calls and he missed an appointment."

"When did it happen?" she asked, looking up at him.

He drew breath and looked away. Shook his head, sighing. "They're not sure yet." He looked at her. Blinked through his

steel-rimmed glasses. "He was on the floor under the shower,"
he said. "Very hot. So they may not be able to tell exactly. The
last time anyone heard from him was late Monday night."

"Oh Lord," she said.

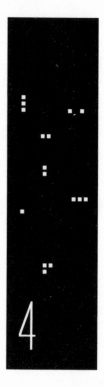

4

Edgar called, of course. "Good God, what abysmally rotten luck!"

"Isn't it, I can't believe it," he said, muting the TV at the foot of the bed. "I spoke to him in the elevator a few times. He seemed like a nice guy." He put the remote on the night table, picked up the I-Heart-New-York mug; held the phone with his shoulder, pushed up the pillows in back.

"And it *had* to be on a day with no news."

"It'll blow over," he said, settling in. "The same as it did with Rafael." He sipped the coffee.

"I beg to differ. This is the fifth, not the fourth, and a somewhat distinguished author, not a superintendent. The building is bound to become—less desirable. I hate to say I told you so, but do you remember my warnings against going rental? If you'd left it a condominium you could be unconcerned. Relatively."

"I know," he said, watching a mute cleanser commercial. "I'm sorry now I didn't listen to you." He sipped coffee.

"I assume you've seen the newspapers."

"Not yet," he said. "I'm still in bed; I was up late last night." He put the mug down, picked up the remote.

"The front page of the *Post* is 'Horror High-Rise' in giant letters, alongside a photo of the building looking up toward the top. The *News* opted for 'High-Rise Horror' with the same layout. The *Times*—here we are—has it on page B three: 'Writer Is Fifth to Die in Upper East Side Building.' They have Connahay working for Merrill Lynch; I suppose they'll correct that tomorrow."

"It'll blow over," he said, thumbing away toddlers, soapflakes, gorillas in the wild. "It'll take a few days longer this time, that's all."

"The phones have been ringing incessantly. 'Who owns the corporation? How do they feel?' "

"Shitty, how do they think?"

"I strongly suggest, and everyone here concurs, that a public-relations specialist be brought in at once."

"To do what?" he asked, thumbing. "Hold a press conference? It'll only keep the story hot."

"No, no, no. To cool the story down. A specialist who would—encourage the media to turn their attention elsewhere as quickly as possible."

He sat up. Asked, "Do you know someone who could do that?"

"I've been told of two people. They're expensive and not necessarily deductible, though I think we could make a persuasive argument to the IRS."

"Fuck the IRS," he said, "get right on it. That's a *great* idea, Edgar. Jesus, what a world we live in."

"I'm glad you agree."

"You bet I do," he said. "Hop to it." He hung up, sat a moment, smiled. Zapped the TV. Slung the blanket off, got up.

Went to the window and threw the right side of it all the way open. Pulled air in through his nostrils, as much of it as he could contain, rising up tall on his toes . . .

Puffed it out, pummeling his bare chest with his fists.

ALEX CALLED, OF course. "I was so sorry to hear the news. Did you know the man?"

"No," she said.

"That's quite a list: a suicide, a cocaine overd—" "Alex, I'm working."

"Oh. Sorry. I just wanted to say hello and see how you're doing."

"Fine," she said. "Wreaths of garlic on the windows, crucifixes close at hand."

"What do you mean?"

"Never mind," she said.

Roxie called. "Jesus, what a pity." Bucked her up. "Chances are he liked all the wrong things."

Vida Travisano rang the doorbell, tinted to perfection and perfumed, pink-nailed fingers holding up the top of an embroidered ivory-satin sheath. She'd gotten the back of it partly buttoned and the fingernails had started coming off.

Kay brought her into the kitchen's white fluorescence, and bending, squinting, teased silk loops over satin pea-buttons. Vida stood pinching her fingertips. Felice, having sniffed Vida's stockinged feet and been patted with the heel of a hand, crouched at her seafood feast.

"Beautiful embroidery . . . India?"

"China. Shit. Do you have Krazy Glue?"

"No, sorry." She looped a button. "Where are you going?" she asked.

"Some dinner at the Plaza," Vida said. "A lot of *speeches* . . . The Governor's going to be there. Isn't it *awful*? Sheer? I spoke to him! In the elevator a few months ago! He had a big plant he got at the street fair on Third Avenue. . . ." She breathed a sigh. "To think of him laying there all that time getting poached. That's what whosit on Channel Five said, *poached*." The blond-capped head turned. "I hope he wasn't a friend of yours or anything. . . ."

She smiled, looping a button. "No, he wasn't," she said.

"Poor guy . . ."

Felice went into the foyer, sat down, began cleaning.

"I knew Naomi Singer," Vida said, pinching a fingernail.

She looped a button, squinting.

"We took a course at the Y," Vida said. "Rape defense. We walked back together a couple of times. You been there? On Lex?"

"To a few concerts," she said.

"They give all kinds of courses. It's a Jewish one but anyone can go."

She said, "She must have been one unhappy lady. . . ."

"She didn't act that way," Vida said, "but I guess they don't always. She was like bubbly on the outside. She had your kind of looks, dark hair, oval face. Not as pretty. Shorter. From 'Baaaston.' Where are you from?"

"Wichita."

"I'm from everywhere," Vida said. "My father's a major general in the Air Force."

Looping a button, she said, "The *Times* didn't say what was in the note. . . ."

"The *Post* had some of it," Vida said. "She was depressed. About everything. The environment, racism, nuclear weapons, you know. And there was a guy in Boston she'd broken up with, he was in it too." She sighed. "She sure scared the pants off Dmitri."

"What do you mean?"

"She nearly hit him," Vida said. "He was polishing the—you know, the rods that hold up the canopy. He was the porter then, Rafael was the super. She landed right alongside him. He had blood on him. The building gave him a week in Disneyland, him and his wife and kid, all expenses paid."

"Not so bad," she said, looping a button.

"Oh, they're not chintzy here," Vida said. "They better not be, with so many people popping off. Who's going to want to renew?" She shook her head, sighed. " 'Horror High-Rise . . .' Yikes. I feel like I'm in a Jamie Lee Curtis movie."

She looped the top button, smiling. "Okay, Jamie Lee," she said, stepping back, "go say hello to the Governor. You look terrific."

A PAISLEY-WRAPPED PACKAGE on the mailroom counter was addressed calligraphically to her, from someplace called Victoriana on East Eighty-ninth Street. About the size of a shoebox, fairly heavy, the Art Nouveau label expensively printed. She wondered who and what as she rode up in the elevator with the goateed man on twelve and a middle-aged Japanese couple who got out on sixteen.

"Who" was Norman and June, Norman's handwriting big and round on the heavy cream card embossed with Diadem's logo: *Clear skies, bright stars, good luck. We love you. Norman and June.*

"What," in a roll of plastic bubble-wrap and deep blue tissue paper, was a magnificent brass telescope, two sections opening out to eighteen or twenty inches, stamped near the eyepiece with a Liberty Bell, the name Sinclair, and the year 1893.

Feeling like Ahab, she watched a tugboat pushing a barge

upriver, a white yacht heading down. Cars moving on the Triboro Bridge. The windows of high-rises, telescopes on tripods standing in some of them. Her knee was rubbed—Felice on the windowsill, purring.

She went with Roxie and Fletcher to the flea market on Twenty-sixth Street, bought a pair of pewter candlesticks; to a revival of *Annie Hall* and *Manhattan*, a Chinese restaurant.

She read a good manuscript. Got a cut and a rinse. Lunched Florence Leary Winthrop at the Seasons. Another man sat where Sheer had sat. She attended a production meeting.

Her at-home day that week, Wednesday, was a stinker, rain drizzling down on the brown park and gunmetal reservoir, on the Jewish Museum's pinnacled slate roof, on brown gardens between black roofs of midblock brownstones. A great day, though, for being at home—even when it meant crawling through Florence's arrow-strewn pages of typing and serpentine handwriting.

A great day too for doing the laundry, she realized as Susannah scrubbed bloodstains from Derek's riding jacket; no wait for the machines. The clock said 3:25. She left Susannah scrubbing and worrying, got the stuffed laundry basket out of the linen closet—Felice came into the foyer to see what was doing—gathered towels from the bathroom and kitchen, Tide from under the sink, quarters from the Mickey Mouse mug.

When she carried the overstuffed basket with the box on top into the white-tiled laundry room, Pete whatever with the reddish-brown hair turned from one of the dryers opposite the door and stood looking at her, something yellow sliding from his hand to his laundry basket. She said, "Hi," going to the side of the room and clomping the basket onto the end washer. Near the other end of the line red lights gleamed on a humming washer with an empty basket on it.

"Hi!" he said, his voice tile-sharpened. "How are you?"

"Fine," she said, sorry she hadn't fixed herself up a little even if he *was* twenty-seven, tops. "You?"

"Fine," Pete *Henderson* said. "Are you all settled in now?"

"Just about." She smiled at him smiling that dynamite smile, in a green T-shirt and jeans—and turned aside, opened the tops of two washers. Taking the filters out, she said, "Isn't this super equipment? Everything's first-rate here."

"It was supposed to be a condo originally," he said, turning to his dryer.

"Lucky for me it isn't," she said.

"Me too."

She put the box aside and began unloading the basket, the colored things into one washer, the white into the other. "I wonder how come it was changed?" she said.

"I guess the demand changed."

"Still," she said, "once they'd made the investment . . . Who owns it, do you know?"

"Uh-uh. All I know is MacEvoy-Cortez, where the checks go." He sighed a resonant tile-bounced sigh. "You sure got a whale of a welcome. . . ."

She said, "You can say *that* again. . . ."

"Aren't those reporters incredible? I suppose they're decent people to begin with, but boy, they sure wind up—piranhas. Like in James Bond. Eat anything."

"He was going to write a book about television," she said, putting a pair of jeans in with the colored, "the different ways it's affected our lives. I wonder if he was going to include that, turning reporters into piranhas."

"Did you know him?" he asked, turning.

She worked at a handkerchief snagged on a shirt button. "Slightly," she said. "We'd been introduced."

"It sounds like a good subject," he said. "I watched all the time when I was a kid; now I just rent movies once in a while. Was he going to include the way VCR's have changed things?"

"I would think so," she said. "He didn't go into details. We only spoke a minute or two."

"It must have made it worse for you though," he said, "having met him."

"Oh sure," she said. "It did. Definitely." She put the shirt in one washer, the handkerchief in the other.

"I talked with him a couple of times about the weather. You know, in the elevator. And I read his book on computers."

"I did too," she said, turning. "What did you think of it?"

He stood silent, frowning. "It was all right," he said. "I thought it was well written but—it annoyed me." He looked at her. "I'm *in* computers," he said. "There's no reason to get paranoid about them; they're machines, that's all, machines that process data quickly."

"He didn't get paranoid," she said. "There are real dangers inherent in them."

"He exaggerated them by a factor of about ten," he said.

She turned. Hand-over-handed the yellow-flowered sheets from the basket down into the white. "What do you do?" she asked.

"I'm a free-lance programmer," he said. "I do consulting for different companies, financial mostly, and I've written some games that have been marketed." The dryer door closed. "You?"

"I'm an editor," she said. "At Diadem Press."

"Would you like a snack? Or a candy bar?" He was going to the vending machines at the other side of the room, looking at her over his shoulder.

"No, thanks." She smiled at him, turned. Sorted the last towels and washcloths.

Coins dropped in a slot. "They've got catnip here, did you know that?"

"Go on," she said, "I didn't." She opened the spout of the Tide.

"Dog chews too. How come no parakeet seed?" A machine hummed; something fell.

Powdering a trail around the colored things, she stopped midway and righted the box, turned. Looked at him coming across the room tearing at a bag. He smiled at her. "I saw you buying litter in Murphy's," he said. "Saturday morning."

"Oh," she said.

"I was with someone," he said, "so I didn't say hello."

She smiled, turned. Trailed out more powder.

He leaned against the humming red-lighted washer, two away from her. "Male or female?" he asked.

"Female," she said. "A calico."

He tore open his bag of potato chips.

"Where are you from?" she asked, circling the box above the white things.

"Pittsburgh," he said. "I've been here five years now. In New York, I mean. Three in the building." He reached toward her, offering the open bag of chips, his vivid blue eyes looking at her.

"No, thanks," she said, smiling, pushing the spout on the box closed. She turned, put it in the basket. "I'm from Wichita," she said. "I've been here—ye gods, eighteen years now."

"I knew you were from someplace in the Midwest," he said. "From the way you speak. It's nice."

She looked at him picking a chip out of the bag. "Thanks," she said.

Put the filters into the washers. Shut their tops.

"Get out your gas mask," he murmured, looking beyond her. She smelled Giorgio as she turned.

The stocky black-banged woman on eight stopped in the doorway, beneath the videocamera, in dark glasses, amber beads, a black long-sleeved dress. Behind her a man wheeled a bike into one of the elevators.

They nodded to her and said, "Hi."

She nodded; went to the vending machines, black high heels clicking on vinyl. Giorgio challenged Tide and Clorox.

Pete sniffed the air, smiled at her. She smiled, plugging quarters into the coin trays. He straightened from the washer— its lights had gone out—and went to the dryers. Coins dropped in slots across the room; machines hummed, things fell.

She homed the trays, studied the glowing selector buttons.

A woman came in and went sniffing and frowning to the

washer Pete had leaned against—a plump black-haired woman in a red blouse and purple skirt, brown scuffs. She took the basket from the washer, opened the top.

"You timed that perfectly. It just went off."

The woman turned to her. "Eh?"

"Just, went, off," she said. "Now." Sliced with a hand. "Off." She pointed at the washer.

"*Ah, sí,*" the woman said, smiling. She pulled matted laundry out into the basket. "*Sí, veintecinco minutos,*" she said. "*Exactamente. Veintecinco minutos.*"

"Twenty-five," she said.

"*Sí.*"

"Thanks."

She touched buttons; the washers rushed to life. She took the box from the basket. "Not yet," Pete said, alongside her with his basket of clean clothes, glancing toward the hallway.

She searched around for *something* until Giorgio, champion over Tide and Clorox, went into an elevator and the door had closed.

"She must have a pipeline from the factory," Pete said as they went into the tan-painted hallway.

"It's Giorgio," she said. "Talk about too much of a good thing." She touched the button between the doors. The indicators above showed 2 become L, 4 become 5.

The stairway door at the right of the elevators opened and Terry in a wet black rubber raincoat came into the hallway. Smiling at them, he went into the laundry room. A man came out of the bike room in a wet yellow poncho, a foam helmet in his hand. He closed the mesh door, nodded at them.

They nodded.

He wiped a hand over damp blond curls, shook it at the floor.

"Still coming down?" Pete asked.

"Worse than before," the man said—fleshy-looking, in his mid-thirties.

The left-hand elevator door slid open.

"Would you?" Pete asked, coming in after her with his laundry basket. "Thirteen." She touched 20, 13. The man in the poncho touched 16.

The door slid open at the lobby and a round-faced elderly woman in a navy hat and raincoat came in; nodded, turned, touched 10.

They rode up in silence. The woman got out.

"Nice seeing you again," Pete said, smiling at her as the door slid open on thirteen.

"Same here," she said, smiling at him.

The man in the poncho got out on sixteen.

She stood holding her box of Tide.

Glanced at the videocamera up in the corner.

Got out her keys as 19 above the door became 20.

SHE HAD A few friends over that Friday night—Diadem people and Roxie and Fletcher. They praised the apartment, Felice, and Roxie's falcon; took turns with the telescope, sipped vodka, soda, white wine; talked about takeover rumors, the Middle East crisis, the spring list.

"That's a beautiful light," June said as they ate. "Is it yours?" Everyone looked up at the ceiling light—the ten or twelve of them and she too, sitting around the living room with their plates of chicken and salad, glasses of wine. "It's the building's," she said, on a cushion by the coffee table. "Everything in the place is first-rate. It was planned as a condo but there's a mysterious owner who switched it to rental. Nobody knows who he is; he hides behind a law firm downtown. Supposedly he's a pain in the ass but in my book he's right up there with Santa Claus."

"This chicken is great," Norman said.

"From Petak's," she said.

"Someone must know who he is," Gary said.

She sipped wine. "The brokers who manage the place don't," she said. "They deal with the lawyers."

"Well, it's not surprising," Tamiko said. "Let's face it, the building hasn't been getting dream publicity."

"This goes back to when he bought it," she said.

"From Barry Beck," June said. "I never thought I'd be sitting here. Did you, Norman? We fought against this building."

"We're active in Civitas," Norman said. "It's an organization that tries to preserve the area and keep it from being overbuilt. There were two beautiful brownstones on this site. We lost the battle but we won the war—against slivers, at any rate. They were outlawed a month after the foundation for this one was poured."

"The construction is certainly first-rate," Stuart said. "I haven't heard a sound from next door and there were people going in there too. My building's a new rental and I can hear my neighbors pushing their phone buttons."

"If it was built to condo standards," Tamiko said, "why did he turn it into a rental?"

"That's what I wondered," she said, going around refilling wineglasses. "It bugged me. I spoke to Jo Harding in accounting—she invests in real estate—and she said the rental market up here has been softer than the condo market for years. So I called the woman who showed me the place and buttered her up a little. She's the one who said he's a pain in the ass, and she only knows he's a man because the lawyers call him a son of a bitch. Felice! Get down from there! Now! He pesters them about the maintenance, blackballs prospective tenants for no logical reason. . . . Fletcher? Just a bit? He acts as if he lives here, but why would he live in a three-room apartment? He's got to be worth at least fifty million. Wendy?"

"He could have a pied-à-terre here," Stuart said, "and live in six other places."

"I suppose so," she said, pouring wine into Wendy's glass, "but she gave the sense of a full-time nuisance."

"Barry Beck probably knows who he is," June said.

"Or the contractor, a man named Michelangelo," Norman said. "Beck sold it when it was still unfinished."

"I'm not that interested in pursuing it," she said, refilling Gary's glass. "I'll assume he's a nut and let him have his privacy; I'm grateful to him. Will everybody please take some more chicken?"

HE SAT STARING. Waggled his head, slack-jawed.

Tried to laugh.

You had to keep your sense of humor, right?

That *she* should be the first one in how-long-had-it-been to look the gift horse in the mouth and ask questions, that her bosses should steer her *instantaneously* toward Michelangelo . . . There had to be a laugh in there somewhere.

"Pain in the ass" and "son of a bitch."

Har-dee-har-har.

He watched her bringing in the strawberry mousse, putting it on the dining table. Wondered if he might be caught someday.

Of course he might. How come he hadn't considered the possibility before? A Columbo clone at the door: "I hate to bother you but could you possibly let me have a couple of minutes of your time? I've got some questions here about the deaths in this building. . . ."

Relax. Stay cool. She wasn't going to pursue it. Hadn't she said so?

And Michelangelo was in Bimini, fishing for sailfish and screwing his new young wife, and would play dumb about anything connected with the building even if it was the Pope asking the questions. So let's not get paranoid.

He got up and got some more ginger ale. Found some chicken lo mein.

Sat eating, watching them sipping decaf and spooning the strawberry mousse, oohing and aahing over it. Nice for her.

He watched Vida's little party, and the Stangersons'.
Chris breaking the news to Sally.
Stefan pleading with Hank.
Kay heading for the foyer with good old Norman and June.
Stay cool. Not to worry.
Hadn't she said she was going to let him have his privacy?

"AM SO SORRY not coming before party," Dmitri said.

"That's all right," she said, showing him into the bedroom. "Scoot, Felice. Go on, scoot."

"Was in boiler room a flood yesterday," Dmitri said, shaking a green-topped spray can near his shoulder.

"Oh my," she said, following him.

"Fixed now. Soon dry. Mmm! Such a nice day!" He put the can on the sill by the end of the desk and tugged with both hands at the window's right-hand inner panel—tugged it open four or five inches. Moved across and tugged the left-hand outer panel open the same. "No problem," he said.

Holding her arms, rubbing them against the chill air, she studied Dmitri in his gray shirt and shiny brown pants as he shook the spray can, pulled its top off. Did fixing tight windows remind him of Naomi Singer doing her swan dive and nearly hitting him? Stupid woman . . . If she'd had to do it, why hadn't she done it from her bedroom?

He seemed untroubled, bending, drawing a plume of spray slowly along the inner track, coming her way. She moved farther aside and back, closer to the closet wall. Asked, "What is that?"

"Silicone," he said, spraying back the other way.

Felice sprang onto the sill and leaned out and down, rump up, white tail waving its black tip, as Dmitri put the can down and took hold of the panel.

Stepping forward, she stroked Felice's back. "No . . ." She picked her up with both hands, lifted her and turned her around, held her in midair, forelegs splayed, the orange-and-white face close to hers. "*No*," she said, staring into the slit-pupil green eyes. "N, O. We do not lean out of windows here. All nine lives, pfft. That's a definite no-no. Capeesh?" Felice looked at her; she looked at Dmitri.

He seemed as untroubled as before, moving the panel toward her. She stepped back, putting Felice on her shoulder; kissed and petted her. Said, "I hear the owner of the building is a pain in the neck." Felice purred.

Dmitri sprayed the farther half of the track. "Meals I know," he said, "not owner."

"Meals?"

"Mr. Meals, manager. You know Mr. Meals. . . ." Dark eyes glanced at her.

"He sent me a letter," she said. "Does he like the marble in the lobby?"

"*Da!* Surprise. Marble is good." He put the can down, pulled the panel to him, slid it from side to side. "See? No problem." He coasted the panel in its easy track, side to side, side to side.

"Terrific," she said. Felice purred at high. Stroking her, she watched Dmitri spray the farther half of the outer track. "Dmitri . . ." she said, "I wonder . . . did Mr. Mills ever tell you to— give extra attention to one tenant, listen to what he says, do what he asks?"

He nodded. "*Da*," he said. "She . . ."

"A woman?" she said.

"You," he said.

"Me?"

He nodded. Put the can down. "When you sign lease." He pulled the outer panel toward him.

She said, "When I *signed the lease?*"

He drew the inner panel over. Glanced at her. "You not know Mr. Meals?" he asked, dark eyes twinkling above his apple cheeks.

"*No*," she said.

He shrugged. "He say, 'Make sure she happy. Take extra good care.' " He picked the can up, shook it.

She lifted Felice from her shoulder, put her down on the rug, looked at him. "You're sure he said *me*," she said.

" 'Meese Norris,' " he said, spraying along the near half of the outer track. " 'Moves into twenty B. Make sure she happy. Take extra good care.' "

"And he doesn't *always* say something like that when—"

Shaking his head, he said, "Never. Never. You only."

She said, "I can't understand how that could be. . . ."

He coasted both panels, side to side, side to side.

He did the living-room window too.

Backed from her moneyed palm with raised hands, holding the spray can. "No, no. Please. Glad. No."

She didn't push it.

Went back to cleaning.

Wendy called to thank her. They talked about how much better June looked. What was going on between Tamiko and Gary.

Tamiko called. They talked about Stuart, Wendy.

June. After the chitchat she said, "June, I do want to find out who owns this building; could you get me the builder's phone number, or the contractor's, or both?"

"Yes, I'm sure Civitas will have them."

"I'm going to call the manager Monday," she said, "but he's in the same office as the woman I spoke to; he probably doesn't know any more than she does. And I don't see the lawyers being forthcoming. I'll let you know for sure Monday. Don't bother till I do."

"What made you change your mind?"

She told her.

"I love it! It's right out of *Lydia's Landlord*."

"*Olivia's Landlord*," she said. "*Lydia's Doctor*."

"Whichever. Do you want to come play Scrabble tomorrow afternoon? It's supposed to rain. Paul's going to be here."

They left it open.

THANK YOU, DMITRI.

No, thank you himself, for telling Edgar to have them take extra good care of her in the first place. As if otherwise somebody might have insulted her or pushed her down a flight of stairs.

No question about what he had to do now, whether he wanted to or not. And before Monday morning.

After Edgar stonewalled and Barry Beck really didn't know, she was going to be on the phone pronto with Dominic Michelangelo. Maybe he'd play dumb but maybe she'd inspire some of his witty macho repartee. *Had she ever been on TV? She sounded pretty enough.* . . . Especially if she caught him with a glass in his hand, which was probably hard not to do nowadays. *Was she sure she'd never been on TV?*

And she would wonder how come he was retired and living in Bimini, still in his forties. . . .

Before *tomorrow* he had to do it. Because tomorrow she could be out all afternoon playing Scrabble and maybe stay there for dinner.

Part of him *wanted* to do it, he knew that. Knew which part of him too. You don't watch a shrink of Dr. Palme's caliber for three years without picking up a few personal insights.

But she'd really left him no choice. The minute she caught on to the cameras she'd be blowing the whistle right and left; no buying off a straight arrow like her. He'd be finished. Charged even with Brendan's heart attack—not that one charge more or less would make a difference.

It was prudence, not paranoia.

He stayed cool. Tracked different approaches while she finished cleaning and went out to shop. Daisy's famous father, in from Washington, was giving Glenn and Daisy the inside scoop on the Middle East crisis. He couldn't focus on it, didn't even bother taping.

Decided on the best way to handle it, thought out the details. Tried to stay cool.

He went out and did some shopping himself, hurrying up Madison, hoping he wouldn't bump into her.

Watched out for her going back in.

She was at her desk, settling down to work on the same manuscript she'd been working on all week.

He put the bottle in the refrigerator.

Watched her. Waited.

He called her at 5:08 by both their clocks, as she finished a short end-of-a-chapter page, Felice snoozing in the middle of the bed. He had them on 1, nothing on 2.

She was turned toward the phone at the window end of the desk when he said who it was; he couldn't see her face, didn't give her time to speak. "I'm sorry to bother you," he said, "but there's something I'd like to speak to you about. It's a little heavy for the phone. It has to do with the building. Could I see you, please, for a couple of minutes?"

"Right now?" she asked, swiveling in the chair, swinging her glasses up into her hair, looking toward Felice standing on the bed arching her back.

"If it's not a bad time for you," he said.

She said, "No, it's not . . ."

"May I come up?" he asked.

She walked the chair closer to the bed as Felice stalked toward her paw by paw. "In ten minutes," she said. Felice flew into her lap. "Oof," she said, swiveling back. "A cat just pounced on me."

Smiling, he said, "It's a jungle out there. Up there, I mean. Thank you."

"See you," she said.

They hung up.

He drew a deep breath. Puffed it out, watching her swinging around in the chair, putting her glasses on the desk, stroking Felice's back. "Hmm . . ." she said. "Interesting . . ."

"You said it," he said.

She switched the lamp off, pulled down the desk's gleaming top. Stood up, dumping Felice to the rug. Went to the closets, unbuttoning her shirt.

Changing for him. Nice . . .

He looked down at his stained jeans.

He'd better change too.

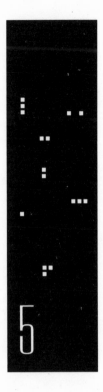

5

She put on the black jeans and the beige turtleneck, black flats.

Brushed her hair and put on lipstick and blush, might as well, wondering what it could be that was a little heavy for the phone and had to do with the building. Something connected with the deaths? She hoped not, didn't want to be reminded of—Humming "Strike Up the Band," she switched the bathroom light off, went through the foyer switching the light on, and into the living room; switched on the end-table lamps.

Dmitri's spray tinged the air. She went to the window and opened the right-hand panel, caught it as it slid too far—good job, Dmitri—pulled it back to a few inches open. The sky was dark; the Matchbox traffic, less of it than on weekdays, flowed and paused in the streetlights' pink-gold glow.

Listening for the elevator door, she went back into the bedroom and eased the left side of the window open. Cool earthy air flowed past her as she returned through the foyer. Felice looked out at her from the kitchen, up on her hind legs scratching at the post. "Good cat, what a cat," she said, veering in. She got the box of treats from the cabinet, shook one out, tossed it. Put the box back and got a treat for herself from the fridge, a cherry tomato from under the salad's wrap. Chewing, she rinsed her fingers, wiped them on the dish towel.

She went into the living room. De-neatened the books and bowl on the coffee table. Raised the blind all the way and cinched it.

Stood watching a long truck, a moving van, jockeying into Ninety-second Street, its ID number black on the pink-gold roof. It hitched back and forth, clogging traffic on the avenue. Horns honked, blatted. Felice meowed.

Stood meowing at the hall door. Meowed at the crack at its bottom.

The bell chimed as she went to the door. She leaned to the peephole; unlocked the door and opened it. "Hi," she said, smiling, offering her hand.

"Hi," Pete said, shaking it, smiling, coming in, in a canary sweater over a white shirt, knife-edged tan chinos, new-looking white sneakers. Felice sniffed them; he crouched down to her, rubbing a hand back over her head and ears. "And here's the famous pouncing cat," he said, rubbing down around the side of her neck. "Isn't she a cutie. . . ." Felice lifted her orange-and-white head, eyes clenched, as he tickled a finger under her jaw. Comb tracks streaked his dampened red-brown hair. "How old is she?"

"Going on four," she said, smiling, closing the door.

"What's her name?"

"Felice."

His blue eyes looked up at her. "As in Felix?" he asked.

"*Yes*," she said, smiling down at him. "You're the second person to catch that in less than twenty-four hours, which is amazing. It goes right past almost everybody."

"Really?" He smiled at Felice pushing the side of her head against his rubbing hand.

"I had company last night and someone got it," she said. "Someone who's known her for over a year."

"It's a great name for a female cat," he said.

"It's Spanish for happy too," she said, "but I wasn't thinking of that."

"Oh sure, *feliz*," he said, standing up. "Hey, that's great. . . Wow, what a painting. That's terrific. . . ."

"My best friend did it," she said.

"Really? No amateur, I'm sure."

"No, she's exhibited here and in Toronto. Roxanne Arvold."

He squinted. "It's great the way she's got the—grace of it," he said, "and the *delicacy* of all the feathers and all, without letting you forget it's a bird of prey."

She said, "That's what she was aiming for. . . ." Looking at him.

He turned toward the living room. "Oh that's nice," he said. "You furnished it very nicely. Great colors . . ."

"There are things that haven't come yet," she said, following after him and Felice.

He stood before the Zwick. "I like this too," he said. "It's got a Hopper feeling. Another friend?"

"No," she said. "The Washington Square art exhibit."

He circled around. "Very nice . . ." he said. Looked at the sofa. "What color would you call that?"

She looked, cocked her head. "Apricot," she said.

"Apricot . . ." He studied it. "Great color . . ."

She smiled at him, and at the sofa. "It was a great sofa too," she said, "before Felice got at it. I'm going to have it refinished and re-upholstered once she's learned to use the scratching post. I have a feeling that the minute I'm in the elevator she's back here scratching the arms again."

"I have a feeling you're right," he said, smiling, bending sideways and scratching Felice's head as she rubbed it against his chinos. "Cats being how they are . . ." He looked around. "Wow," he said, standing straight. "What a difference between thirteen and twenty." He went to the window, looked out through the right-hand panel. "This is fantastic. I've got the roof of the Wales and the back of that building."

"Be careful," she said, going to the window. "They slide easily. Dmitri sprayed the tracks this morning."

"Is that Queens or Brooklyn?" he asked.

"Queens," she said, looking out through the left-hand panel.

He whistled. "What a view," he said, bowing Felice's tail as she walked the windowsill.

They stood looking out at glittering high-rises, blue and gold bridge lights doubled in water, far-off fields of light. Stars gleamed in the dark above, a few of them moving, red and white. "JFK is out that way," he said.

She said, "What did you want to speak to me about?"

He turned toward her, drew a breath, his blue eyes troubled. "I've been feeling guilty," he said. "The other day, in the laundry room, you asked me if I knew who owned the building, and I said no. I think maybe you're still wondering about it, because of what you said about why was it changed to rental after the money had been invested." He smiled. "I have a feeling you're the kind of person who . . . doesn't give up on a puzzle until she's got it solved." He shrugged. "And I don't like to think that maybe you're being distracted from your work for no good reason."

She said, "You know who owns it?"

He nodded.

"Who?" she asked.

He touched his canary-sweatered chest, tapped it with a finger. "Me," he said. "I'm the owner."

She looked at him.

"I semi-grew-up in the neighborhood," he said. "My folks had an apartment over on Park besides the house in Pittsburgh. *And* the house in Palm Beach . . ." He sighed, smiled. "I inherited a load of loot when I was twenty-one," he said. "I always liked living here the best of all, so I moved into the Wales while I sort of got my bearings. Five years ago that was. Listen, Kay—is it all right if I call you Kay?"

Nodding, she said, "Sure . . ."

"Would you mind if I closed this window?" he asked. "It's a little chilly standing here."

"Oh sure, go ahead," she said. "And sit down, for goodness' sake."

He closed the window.

She sat on the near end of the sofa, a leg folded under her.

He sat in a side chair, crossed his legs, loosed the pressed knee of his chinos.

Felice curled up on a cushion by the heating strip below the window. Watched them.

"So as I said," he said, leaning toward her with an elbow on the chair arm, his hands folded, "there I was in the Wales. Sixth floor front, watching them demolish the brownstones that used to be here, two of them, and excavate, and pour the concrete. . . . And it hit me that it would be really cool to own an apartment house and live in it, since I enjoyed the time I spent in Eleven-eighty-five so much. That's where we were—the big building with the drive-in courtyard?"

She nodded.

"And real estate is a good investment, isn't it? It's how Donald Trump started." He smiled. "So I had my lawyers buy it," he said. "I switched it to rental because if it were a condo and somebody turned out to be a pain, gave noisy parties every night or something, I'd be stuck with them. This way I've got some flexibility. And I don't let anyone know I'm the owner, not even the folks at MacEvoy-Cortez, believe it or not, because I don't want to be bothered about the details and have people coming to me with complaints, and the staff kissing my ass all the time, excuse the expression."

She said, "You live here all year round?"

He nodded. "I'm a computer person," he said. "I'm not interested in yachts and mansions. Oh, I expect one day I'll get a bigger place to live in, with a game room and maybe a pool, but right now a small apartment suits me fine. I can take care of it myself without having anyone fussing with my papers and things."

"How come you didn't take the whole top floor?" she asked, smiling. "That's what I'd have done."

He smiled. "I told you," he said, "I'm a computer person. I spend the day looking at my monitor, and most of the night too; the view would be totally wasted. So I'm on thirteen. It's the hardest floor to rent. You'd be surprised how many people are superstitious."

"Especially now," she said.

He nodded. "Especially now." He sighed.

She said, "It's a tough break for you. Has the building lost value?"

He shrugged. "A little, maybe. It'll come back up."

She smiled at him. "You were right," she said, "I was still wondering. I even asked Mrs. MacEvoy, the day after we spoke."

"You did?" he said.

"I feel a little—tacky about it now."

"No, don't be silly," he said. "It's great you have that kind of persistence. I said, I sensed it about you."

They smiled at each other.

"Would you like a drink?" she asked.

"Sure, why not?" he said. "Thanks. A gin and tonic?"

"Vodka?" she asked, getting up.

"Fine," he said. Looked across the room. "You certainly have a lot of books. How many of those are ones you edited?"

She stopped beyond the sofa. "Pete," she said, turning, "Dmitri said he was told to take special care of me. When I signed the lease. Why?" She stood looking at him.

He drew a breath. Uncrossed his legs and leaned forward, forearms on knees. "Thank you, Dmitri," he said.

Turned his head, looked at her. Nodded. "When you came to look at the apartment," he said, "I happened to be in the mail room. I saw you for a moment."

"A moment?" she said, smiling.

He said, "Did you ever hear of a television actress named Thea Marshall?"

She looked at him.

He sat straight, stared at her, his blue eyes electric. "Oh my God," he said, "I just realized. Of *course* you've heard of her, people must have told you *lots* of times you look like her. I didn't think of it 'til just this instant. Jesus . . ." He shook his head, smiled, got up. "They have, haven't they?" He came toward her. "Told you? Not so many nowadays, I guess."

She said, "Sometimes . . ."

"Your voice is like hers too." He leaned at her over the sofa, gripping its Cupid's-bow back, smiling his dynamite smile. "So a moment was all it took for me to be attracted," he said, "as I'm sure you've noticed. Dr. Palme says it's universal, no exceptions whatsoever. The Oedipus complex, I mean. She was my mother. Thea Marshall." He nodded, smiling. "My mother." He nodded. "Thea Marshall." He blinked, smiled. "I heard him say that in the elevator once," he said. "Dr. Palme in two A. He's a psychiatrist, a good one. On the staff of Mount Sinai."

She looked at him. Raised two fingers. Said, "Two vodka and tonics . . ."

Went into the kitchen.

Drew a breath.

Got glasses from the cabinet.

He came to the pass-through and leaned in, canary-sweatered arms folded on the counter. Watched as she put crescents of ice into the glasses. "She was a terrific actress," he said. "So lifelike you wouldn't believe it. She was on all the great dramatic shows of the Golden Age—*The U.S. Steel Hour, Kraft Theatre, Philco Playhouse, Studio One.* . . . They have kinnies of three of her plays at the Museum of Broadcasting. Kinescopes. Paul Newman has bit parts in two of them. Hi there, Felice."

Felice meowed, going to the water bowl.

She poured vodka over the ice.

"She was on *Search for Tomorrow* most of the time I was growing up," he said. "Play production had moved out to the West Coast and my father wouldn't let her go out there, so she had to do soaps—*The Guiding Light* and then *Search for Tomorrow*. What a job that is. Rehearse in the morning, tape, block tomorrow's show, come home and study the lines; rehearse, tape, block, study—an endless cycle. Practically the only time I saw her was on the tube! She was a fantastic actress though. So lifelike. A year on *The Guiding Light* and six on *Search for Tomorrow* . . ."

She poured tonic. "What did your father do?" she asked.

"He was the chairman of U.S. Steel," he said.

She glanced at him.

He smiled. "I know what you're thinking," he said. "That maybe he used his influence to get her parts on the show. He didn't, not on the *Steel Hour* or *Kraft Theatre*—he owned a lot of Kraft too. But he didn't. He always maintained a strictly hands-off policy where her career was concerned, they both wanted it that way. She never needed help getting good parts, she was a really terrific actress."

She cut lime.

Asked, "Do you have any brothers and sisters?"

"No," he said. "Do you?"

"A younger brother." Felice scratched at the post, looking up at her. "Good cat," she said, turning to the cabinet.

"Don't give her something just like that," he said. "Make her do some serious scratching. She's conning you."

Holding the open cabinet door, she looked at him; at Felice on her hind legs, paws on the post, looking up at her. Giving a scratch to cue her. "You're right," she said, closing the door.

"Sorry, Felice," he said.

Felice looked at him. At her. At him.

They chuckled.

Felice dropped from the post and sauntered into the foyer, black-tipped tail swaying.

"I think I've made an enemy," he said.

"She'll get over it," she said, smiling. "You're right, I've been an absolute patsy. She's so damn smart. . . ." She handed him a glass through the pass-through.

"Thanks." He held the glass toward her. "Cheers," he said.

"Cheers," she said, touching hers to it.

They smiled at each other, sipped.

She turned and went toward the door, saying louder, *"It can't just be a coincidence that Sam Yale is in the building."* Glass smashed on parquet, liquid splashed. She stopped.

"Shit, I'm such a klutz. . . ."

"Don't worry," she said, putting her glass down, going for the paper towels. *"That's another thing you're the second person to do in less than twenty-four hours."*

The border of the rug was wet, and the cuffs of his chinos. Crouching, they blotted at the parquet with paper towels, picked pieces of glass from the puddle. Felice came and watched.

"I'm sorry about the glass," he said.

"I'll deduct it from the rent," she said.

They smiled, blotting the parquet.

"No," he said, "it's not a coincidence that Sam Yale lives here. Are you friends?"

"Acquaintances," she said. "He followed me onto the checkout line at Murphy's the day I moved in."

"I figured you'd meet sooner or later."

"It couldn't have been much sooner," she said. Glanced at him. "Was it just by chance that *you* were on hand to welcome me?"

He smiled. "No comment," he said. Teased a sliver of glass from the floor, set it on paper towel. "There are factors involved in his being here," he said, "that I don't think it would be right for me to go into."

"He told me he's a recovering alcoholic," she said, "and about the foundation."

He looked at her.

"The one supporting him," she said. "Carnegie Hill something. You must know."

He said, "Just like that, in Murphy's?"

"In the park one day."

"Oh."

They wiped the floor.

"Well in that case," he said, "I guess there's no reason why I can't tell you the whole story."

They brought the wet towels and wrapped glass into the kitchen. He took the garbage out to the chute while she made another drink.

They went into the living room.

Sat at the ends of the sofa facing each other, each with a folded leg on the cushion. Reached glasses and clinked them, smiling.

He drank. Looked at his glass. "I think they were lovers," he said. "I don't hold it against him. If he made her happy, fine. My father asked for it. He was a real bastard and had plenty of affairs himself."

She watched him as he drew a breath, took a sip of his drink.

"After she died," he said, "Sam dropped out of sight, for almost ten years. At least you didn't see his credit anywhere. The first I heard of him was a few months after I bought the building; he was speaking down at the New School. 'Directing in Television's Golden Age.' I went to hear him, of course. It was pretty embarrassing. He was half drunk, rambled all over the place, forgot the question he was answering. . . ."

She sighed, shook her head.

"I did some checking," he said. "He was living in a ratty little hole on Bleecker Street, teaching acting. He'd been canned by some school down there. I thought maybe he wouldn't take anything if he knew it was my father's money, so I had my lawyers set up the foundation. It's not a big deal. And they hired someone who got in touch with him and put him into the Smithers Treatment Center, right around the corner. When the building was finished, the foundation rented an apartment for him."

She said, "That was incredibly generous and sensitive of you, and continues to be."

He shrugged. "He directed some of Thea Marshall's best performances," he said. "I knew she would have wanted to help him even if they weren't lovers. And as I said, I don't hold it against him if they were."

"Obviously you don't," she said.

They smiled at each other, drank.

"Well," he said, "we went off on a couple of tangents, but that's what I wanted to tell you, that I'm the owner, so you can stop wondering. I told you another lie down there. I knew you had a cat from your application, I wasn't in Murphy's with anyone last Saturday morning. I took a chance that that was when you shopped and that you bought litter."

She smiled at him. "You're a good guesser," she said. "Both lies forgiven. Gladly."

They drank.

Felice jumped up on the sofa between them. Walked the yielding apricot velvet and sniffed his rubbing fingers. He caressed her head. "Everybody's forgiving me," he said.

She looked at him. Said, "Aren't you afraid I'll tell the other tenants?"

"No," he said. He shook his head. "You won't. You'll—protect my privacy."

"How do you know?" she asked.

He shrugged. "I just know it." His vivid blue eyes looked at her. "That's the kind of person you are," he said. "Do I read you wrong?"

She shook her head, looking at him. "No," she said, "you don't."

They drank.

Felice curled up against his knee. He fingered her orange ear, caressed her head. Said, "What a cutie . . ."

She said, "Are you hungry? I have a refrigerator full of

chicken tarragon and salad, and some super strawberry mousse. . . ."

"That sounds great," he said, smiling at her. "*I've* got a bottle of vintage Dom Perignon champagne, the kind James Bond used to drink. Should I run downstairs and get it?"

She smiled at him. "Why not?" she said.

"ALEX IS SIXTEEN years older than I am. He teaches architectural history at NYU. He was on the faculty at Syracuse when we started going together. In my sophomore year."

"Hotter?"

"Sure."

He took an arm from around her, groped, found the shower handle; turned the water hotter.

"We didn't get married till I was twenty-nine," she said. "Mmm, that's great. And Jeff is *twelve* years older; you're not the only one with a parental hang-up." She kissed his throat as he licked water from her eyebrow. He said, "At least you're getting over yours. . . ." They kissed, laughing.

Kissed. "Oh God . . ." Turned, kissing. "We're going to make *The Guinness Book of Records*. . . ." "Back up . . ." "Wait a sec . . ." She took an arm from around him, groped, found the shower handle; turned the water hotter.

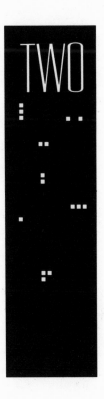

6

She sailed into the office and slowed and walked. Smiled and said good morning—to Gary, to Carlos, to Jean, to Sara—trying to look as if she hadn't spent Saturday night and all day Sunday making rapturous love with a twenty-six-year-old man who happened to be the most perceptive, sensitive, intuitive person she had ever known.

Telling Roxie was one thing; she wasn't about to tell the world.

She looked in on June around ten-thirty, asked how the Scrabble had gone and told her not to bother getting those phone numbers; she had spoken to the manager, there had been a misunderstanding. He had told the super, whose English wasn't very good, to be more attentive to *all* the tenants; so she was going back to her let-the-owner-have-his-privacy position. Life hadn't imitated *Olivia's Landlord* after all. But thanks.

She didn't like lying to June, not even white-lying, but she was afraid that once she got started on how she learned who the owner was, she would wind up gushing out everything.

She had gushed to Roxie on the phone the night before. "He has these vivid blue eyes and I swear to God he sees right into me! And not just me, Roxie; he took one look at the falcon, which he loves, and he *immediately* saw what you were going for and expressed it in *almost exactly your terms*! He even psyched out Felice! You can't *believe* how perceptive he is! And funny, and sweet, and wild about me . . ."

She had told Roxie who his mother had been, and his father, how unaffected he was about his wealth—doing his own laundry, his apartment furnished in simple Conran's contemporary under a layer of mess. . . .

She knew it wasn't going to be a long-term relationship, not with thirteen years between them—and didn't want it to be, for his sake; he ought to have children. But for a while at least, for both of them, it was surely the best possible thing that could have happened.

Roxie, delighted for her, had agreed.

Would Dr. Palme agree too? She hoped so—and that Pete would very soon be secure enough in the relationship to tell her he was in therapy. How could he *not* have been scarred, poor baby, hardly seeing his mother at all except on television?

Though there was, of course, a slight chance, *very* slight, that he *had* overheard the doctor talking in the elevator about the Oedipus complex—between the lobby and the second floor. About one in a million?

In her office, looking out at buildings of glass-walled offices, she longed to call him—just a quick hello to confirm his reality up there on Carnegie Hill.

No. She resolved she wouldn't be a nuisance; he'd be busy at

his computer in that messy Conran's living room, working on
the program he was doing for Price Waterhouse.

She got to work too; buzzed Sara and asked her to bring in
her notebook.

HE WATCHED SAM.

Jabbing with two fingers at the crummy-looking portable he'd
brought back from Tucson. Abe's, probably. He'd set it up on
the living-room table along with a pad of paper and a dictionary;
sat with his glasses on, in his Beethoven sweatshirt, jabbing,
stopping and scratching his ear, jabbing, checking the dictionary. No joint in sight.

Quitting again? And writing what?

The old scumbag . . . On the checkout line behind her the
day she moved in. Trying to repeat history . . .

And in the park! When? How come? What else had he told
her, what had she told him? Obviously they'd had more than a
casual conversation.

The morning after the Rocky thing? When he'd slept till
almost noon and there she was, at the desk, telling Sara how
gorgeous the park had been? Maddening, not to know . . .

He smiled at himself—spoiled by too much knowing. Did it
matter what they'd said, when and how they'd met? Not in the
least. Not a microdot.

Tough, Sammy, you can't win 'em all. Be glad you're alive.
You don't know how lucky you are that Abe didn't get to go to
your funeral. . . .

He watched Beth searching Alison's dresser drawers. Not even
warm.

Dr. Palme and Michelle—the usual. Lisa doing aerobics.

Them again on her bed, she on top, both of them near
coming.

Fantastic, how great she was. Naomi had been frigid by comparison.

He fast-forwarded through a stretch of talking, whizzing them all over the bed, out of the room, back.

Watched them starting in again, kissing, stroking each other.

Thought about calling her, didn't want to bother her.

But she would be feeling the same way. More so. And it wasn't as if she was in rehearsal or on camera . . .

He killed the sound. Called Information for Diadem's number.

. Got to Sara and said, "Hello, my name is Peter Henderson. May I speak to Ms. Norris if she's free? It's a personal matter."

"Just a moment, please."

He watched them lying curled together, sixty-nining.

"Hi . . ."

"Hi . . ." he said, smiling, watching them. "Sorry to bother you but I had to make sure you're real. . . ."

IT WASN'T UNTIL a few days later—when she left the apartment in the morning to find Vida in a flowered kimono hauling out pink suitcases, bound for a month in Portugal and seeming grim about it—that she realized (riding down in the elevator with the blond couple on fourteen, the goateed man on twelve, the black/white couple on seven) that Pete knew the occupation, income, age, and marital status of everyone in the building, and other information too from their credit reports and references.

Talk about fun . . .

She mentioned it that night over burgers and fries at Jackson Hole, around ten.

He sat chewing, looking at her across the small square table.

He swallowed. Sipped from his mug of beer as she took a bite of her burger.

He wiped his lips with his napkin. "I wouldn't say *fun*," he said, "but there's certainly a satisfaction in knowing the basic facts about everybody. We're all curious about our neighbors; it's a defensive instinct from the most primitive part of the brain. Like Felice sniffing." He took a fry from the plate between them.

She said, "It's a lot easier to satisfy the instinct in suburban Wichita, I can tell you that. I grew up knowing everyone on Eleanor Lane and their complete family histories." She took a fry.

He chewed, swallowed. "If you have any questions," he said, "I'll be glad to answer them."

"Thought you'd never ask," she said. "What does Vida Travisano do? My 'hallmate.' "

He smiled. "Officially she's a model," he said. "My lawyer thinks she's a high-price call girl. What's your opinion?"

"Either or both," she said. "I was hoping you'd settle it for me. How come you okayed her? I'm not objecting, she's perfectly sweet, but if your lawyer felt that way . . ."

He took a sip of beer. "I like the idea of having a mix of people in the building," he said. "As much of a mix as you can get, in this neighborhood, at these rents. I don't want to be *entirely* surrounded by yuppie clones, not even in the elevator."

"That sounds reasonable," she said.

"Ah, but you're not a lawyer," he said. "Or someone in real-estate management. I'm sure they think I'm nuts and a pain in the ass."

She smiled at him. Shrugged. "If they do," she said, "that's *their* problem."

They ate bites of their burgers. Played some footsie.

She said, "What are the Johnsons like?"

"The Johnsons?" he said. "Oh, thirteen B. They're never here so I forgot about them. Almost never, a few weeks a year. They're British, fifty-something. He's a lawyer, excuse me, a barrister, and she's—I forget what she does. Nothing. Shops. Comes in with lots of packages."

Giorgio went by outside the window with a German shepherd; stood waiting while it nosed the base of the corner streetlight.

They smiled at each other. "What does *she* do?" she asked.

"Owns a travel agency," he said. "Over on Lexington. Single." He took a fry.

She squinted out the window. "She looks like a man in drag," she said.

He smiled, poking the tip of the fry into ketchup. "You're right, she does," he said. Ate the red-tipped fry, looking away for the waitress.

SHE WENT TO a Women's Media Group lunch at the Harvard Club. Everyone said she never looked better. Ditto at the Vertical Club.

She took Felice to Dr. Monsey on Bank Street for her shots; stopped in at the superette and the bookshop. Everyone said she never looked better.

They biked in the park. Made spaghetti and clam sauce.

Went with Roxie and Fletcher to a Cajun place in SoHo. Pete spoke knowledgeably with Roxie about the artistic process, with Fletcher about federal guidelines in medical-research funding. He told a joke that left them limp. Traded tastes with her, loving looks.

"Didn't I tell you?" she said in the loo.

"Listen," Roxie said, standing on tiptoes at the sink, painting her eyes in the mirror, "if he's rich too and the sex is so great, for God's sake *grab* him!"

"Roxie . . ."

"Steffi is *fifteen* years older than Mike and they're happy as clams. Pounce!"

One night, when he was staying over and they were going to

sleep, she mentioned that an agent was taking her to lunch the next day at the Four Seasons.

"Thea Marshall took me there for my tenth birthday," he said, lying spooned behind her, clasping her breasts, his cheek in her hair. "God, was it impressive for a kid, the scale of it. . . . We were alongside the pool. The waiters and captains all fawning over us, everyone looking . . . Like we were Mary and Jesus . . . Is it some kind of book-people's place now?"

She said, "Just at lunch. The Grill Room."

"I thought I heard that somewhere. . . ."

Felice turned around against their blanketed feet.

She fingered the backs of his hands. "You always refer to her as 'Thea Marshall,' " she said—his hands twitched—"never as 'my mother' . . ."

He shrugged against her. "That's how I think of her," he said. "How I always have. It was the way she *wanted* to be thought of—the actress, not somebody's mother. She only had me because my father made her. And the ironic thing is, she was this really terrific young mother who always did the right thing. On *Search for Tomorrow*. And totally believable. Day after day, a really fantastic performance. I took cabs home from school to catch it, it was before VCR's."

She drew his hands tighter to her, kissed them. Said, "You know, don't you, darling, that there's nothing you can't tell me. . . ."

He lay still against her back. "What do you mean?"

She turned herself around in his arms, hugged him. He stared at her in the near-dark. She kissed the tip of his nose. Said, "Isn't there something you haven't told me, baby?"

He stared at her.

"There's no shame attached to it if you need it," she said. "I'm all for it, you must know that."

Staring, he said, "What are you talking about?"

She said, "Dr. Palme . . ."

He swallowed, looked at her. "Dr. Palme?" he said.

She nodded.

"You—think I—see him?"

She said, "Don't you?"

He looked at her, shook his head. "No," he said. "I'm not his patient. Haven't been. His or anyone's. Why did you think so? When I said I heard him . . . ?"

She nodded. "It seemed so—unlikely," she said. "That he was talking about the Oedipus complex in the elevator, and that you of all people overheard him."

He smiled. Let out breath. "But it happened," he said. Smiled wider. "One of life's amazing coincidences."

She hugged him, nuzzled into his shoulder, giggling. "Oh God, darling, I'm sorry," she said. "*Believe* me, it wasn't anything else! Only that. Oh Lord. That'll teach me a lesson. I was so sure . . ."

They kissed, hugging. Felice jumped off the bed.

He laughed, hugging her. Drew a deep breath, puffed it out over her shoulder. "Jeez," he said, "I couldn't imagine what the hell you were talking about!"

They took the Circle Line cruise around Manhattan.

She trimmed his hair.

He gave her a Tiffany package, the paper the blue of his eyes. The fluid gold openwork heart on a chain, the big one.

She gave him five pounds of gourmet jelly beans—luscious colors.

SAM CALLED. "How are you?"

"Fine," she said. "You?"

"Okay. I was in Arizona for a while. My brother died."

"Oh, I'm sorry to hear it. . . ."

"Yeah, well, what are you gonna do. . . . That was awful about your friend Sheer. I'm beginning to think there's really a jinx on this place."

"Hardly," she said.

"Listen, I did some thinking out there, about what you said. The memoirs. I decided to give it a shot. Funny and serious both, why be shy?"

"Hey, that's *great* news, Sam," she said. "I'm really glad to hear it. I'm sure you can do it."

"Thanks, I hope so. I've written—I guess you'd call it a first chapter. Would you like to see it?"

She drew breath. "I don't think I'm the right one," she said, "I do very little nonfiction; but yes, send it to me, just drop it off in the mail room; I'll get it to an editor who'll be sympathetic to the material and who'll give you a good objective reaction."

"Okay . . . Thanks. That'll be fine, I appreciate it. The typing's from hunger."

"As long as it's double-spaced and legible."

She told Pete about it when he came up—late, he'd hit a glitch in the program he was working on. "It'll be interesting," he said, sitting on the side of the bed after she'd gotten back into it. "Maybe I'll finally find out for sure about him and Thea Marshall."

She watched him untying a sneaker, sparring with Felice over the laces. She said, "I got the impression that there *was* a relationship, and it was very much love-hate. He's liable to say unkind things about her."

He shrugged, glanced at her. "Is that why you're giving it to someone else?" he asked.

"No," she said. "You know I don't do much nonfiction."

He pulled the sneaker off. "It was your idea," he said. "I would think you'd *want* to work on it."

She gathered the manuscript she'd been reading into its box. "Oh boy," she said, shaking her head. "Yes, I would love to, if what he's written is halfway good. But I wouldn't be comfortable working with him now, knowing about you and the foundation when he doesn't, being one-up on him that way. It should be a very open and candid relationship, especially with a writer who'll probably have to be nursed along chapter by chapter. It's no good if I have to watch what I'm saying." She closed the box.

"And yes," she said, "there would be a problem if he got into things I thought might hurt you. . . ." She put the box on the others under the night table.

He was sitting up looking at her when she sat straight.

She smiled at him, reached, caressed his cheek. "It's not important, baby," she said. "Really. I wouldn't even know him if you hadn't brought him here, right?"

He nodded.

She smiled. "So quit stalling and get the clothes off," she said.

He smiled at her. Bent to his other sneaker.

Sam left an envelope in the mail room—folded pages, a dozen. Bad typing but good stuff: New York in the early thirties, eight-year-old Sam and twelve-year-old Abe—Yellen, not Yale—being spirited from the Bronx by Uncle Maurice the actor and shoved onstage in the Group Theatre production of *Waiting for Lefty*.

Slightly E. L. Doctorow . . .

She gave it to Stuart.

IT WAS THE one thing he hadn't expected, that he'd fall in love with her.

Amazing, that lack of foresight, considering how marvelous she was: warm, smart, honest, funny, sexy—and looking like Thea Marshall. All of which he had known almost since the day she moved in—nowhere near as well as he knew it now, of course—yet the thought he might fall in love with her hadn't even crossed his mind.

There it was, though. Ruining everything.

He watched her sitting on the sofa with her glasses on and her feet on the coffee table, reading another manuscript some agent was hot on. Contemporary sexual conflicts.

He wished he could tell her about Phil and Lesley and Mark, Vida, the Fishers, the Hoffmans—about *everything* that was going on in the building, not just the sexual conflicts. How right she had been: it was no good watching every word, having secrets that couldn't be shared. No good? Make that rotten, Kay.

And if Naomi, who hadn't been half as sharp as she was, had caught on, wouldn't *she* catch on sooner or later no matter *how* careful he was? Wasn't he bound to make a slip he couldn't explain someday? What *then*, for God's sake?

She turned, looked at him over her glasses. "What is it?" she asked.

"Nothing," he said. Smiled. "I was just watching you. Resting my eyes."

Smiling, she said, "If you don't like it, don't read it. I won't be hurt."

"No, I'm enjoying it," he said, lifting the open book. "This part on the boat is terrific."

They smiled at each other. She nodded toward the door, chuckling. "Go on downstairs," she said. "Work on the program. I could use some alone time too."

He tucked the book's flap in its pages. "I'm going to take it with me," he said. Leaned to her as she took her glasses off. He kissed her. "I love you," he said.

She kissed him, caressed his cheek, looking at him.

They kissed, and he got up and went around the sofa to the foyer. "*Good night, Felice,*" he called, "*wherever you are!*"

Watching him, she said, "Hey, wait a minute . . ." She put the manuscript aside, getting up.

He waited by the hall door.

She went and stood before him. Looked him in the eye. "One of our editors, Wendy Wechsler," she said, "I think I mentioned her—"

He nodded.

"She does a Thanksgiving dinner for transplanted people who aren't going home," she said. "Would you like to go with me? I know it's late but—I waffled. You know . . ."

He glanced away, drew a breath. Put the book under his arm and took her by the shoulders. "I would *love* to, Kay," he said, "and I appreciate your asking me. Sincerely. But I have these cousins in Pittsburgh that I promised I'd go to. I've been putting them off year after year and I just *can't* back out now after I finally said yes."

She said, "I understand."

"I'm sorry," he said.

"It's okay," she said. "I shouldn't have waited so long."

They kissed. Hugged.

He looked at her. "Ummm . . . ?"

"No, go on," she said. "We both could use a little space. Go on. We'll talk tomorrow."

They kissed.

He opened the door, went out.

She watched him open the stairway door and go out to the landing. He waved at her through the wired-glass panel as the door closed.

She closed the apartment door, turned the bolt. Breathed a sigh. Crouched and picked up Felice. Held her before her, eye to eye. "Cousins?" she asked.

"IS IT ANYTHING I said?"

"No."

"Or did?"

"*No*," he said. "It's me, not you. Honestly." His eyelids closed.

She kissed his lips, smoothed his hair back with both hands. "Something with your work?" she asked.

"No," he said. "Yes. *No*."

"I'm not *completely* computer-illiterate, you know. . . ."

"Honey, please, shh, let's not talk, okay? Shh. Zap, we're mute."

She kissed his lips, his eyelids. Closed her eyes.

He moved in her, stiffening.

■　　　■　　　■

SHE SIGNED A writer, bought a suit.

He didn't call. She decided she'd wait this time.

Worked out at the club, scored at an editorial meeting. Went to a party. Went home and checked the machine. He hadn't called.

She baked two pumpkin pies, Felice watching.

She called the folks Thanksgiving morning. Bob and Cass were there, Uncle Ted, everyone cheery except the baby wailing in the den. A good call—no arguments, no questions about men. They looked forward to her Christmas visit; she did too.

The turkey was dry but the trimmings were great, the table bigger than last year's—familiar faces, new ones. She imagined him at a cold table in a Pittsburgh mansion, or, she hoped, alone at his computer with a frozen dinner, the hell with him. Wendy's suave orthopedist came on to her but she was through with *old* no matter what. The pies were a smash. She went home and checked the machine; he hadn't called.

Friday was dreary—surprise. A gray sky, flecks of snow. She paid some bills, cleaned a little, changed the bed. Got the telescope; watched gulls on the reservoir, joggers on the mesh-fenced track—two middle-aged women arguing on the shoulder, one showing her palms, the other shaking a finger, both in blue sweatsuits. Too bad she couldn't lip-read. Felice, on the window-sill, nuzzled her knee.

She tried to do some work—paring down an overstuffed bio of Dorothy Parker. Got nowhere with it. What was *he* doing?

She cocooned herself on the sofa and watched soaps—*One Life to Live, General Hospital*. Hoped the actresses, fairly decent, some of them, were giving their kids enough quality time. Roxie called; she kept her mouth shut and listened for a change. Said everything was fine, status quo. Busy.

She watched *Now, Voyager*, Felice sleeping in her lap.

Ate a yogurt, took a bath.

On Saturday she got back on track; put the TV in its corner, finished the cleaning, shopped, squared herself at the desk. Three weeks since the whole thing had started. She polished his open gold heart with her thumb—and got to work. Picked up speed, plowed ahead. Clean copy, thank God.

The phone rang as she finished marking a short end-of-a-chapter page—4:54 on the clock. She watched the phone. It rang. She picked up. "Hello?" she said.

"Hi."

She took her glasses off. "Hi," she said.

"How was Thanksgiving?"

"Caloric," she said. "Fun. Yours?"

"I didn't have one. I was lying, I was afraid we were getting in too deep. I'm sorry now."

She turned in the chair. "So am I," she said.

"I love you, Kay."

"Oh Petey"—she shut her eyes, drew breath—"*I* love *you*, baby, so much. . . ."

"Oh honey . . . God, I've missed you. There's something we have to talk about, it's too heavy for the phone. Does that sound familiar?"

Smiling, she said, "Two vodka and tonics, coming up."

"No. Down here this time. Would you mind?"

"Terribly," she said. "Now?"

"Whenever you're ready."

"Fifteen minutes."

"You won't know the place. I cleaned in your honor."

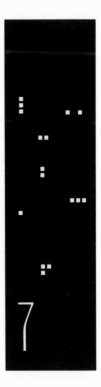

7

Whatever it was, they could deal with it, now that he was ready to talk about it. The damn age difference, probably.

She showered and made herself gorgeous and thirty-five, tops. Put on white slacks and flats and the peach pullover, the heart on the chain. Florence Leary Winthrop called, manic, wanting to bounce ideas off her; it took five minutes to get a postponement till first thing Monday. She turned the machine on, got her keys. Put down fresh food and water, told Felice she'd see her later.

The elevators were at fifteen and six, both going down; she

took the stairs. Jigged down the zigzagging half-flights lit by fluorescents at the numbered landings, her footfalls whispering down the gray concrete well. She hoped it *was* the age difference, not MS or cancer or something, there in that bad-luck building. . . .

She went out on thirteen.

He was busy in the kitchen in a plaid shirt and jeans, the apartment door wide open, the Beatles singing "Hey Jude." He turned, smiling the dynamite smile. "Two vodka and tonics," he said, wiping his hands on a hanging towel. "But I'm sorry, miss, you'll have to show me some ID. . . ."

They kissed through the end of "Hey Jude," a deejay talking, and part of "Eleanor Rigby."

She went into the living room, combing her hair with her fingers. The blind was down, cups of light on chrome rods glowed at the ceiling; the ceiling light glowed back. The tan-carpeted room looked sterile—a bit—minus its overlay of clothes and what-all. But nice, the tan leather couch almost at the center, facing the TV and stereo at the left; the desk and computer against the right-hand wall, table and chairs by the pass-through—everything tan and white and chrome except some yellow and orange cushions, the twinkling red stereo lights, the black TV.

"It looks *great*," she said. "You're right, I wouldn't have recognized it."

"I took out a ton of stuff," he said, going to the couch with two glasses, ice tinkling. "Suddenly I have glasses again."

She checked the low bookcase by the desk—technical books and texts, some in Carnegie-Mellon jackets. *The Worm in the Apple* stood among them.

The Beatles stopped as he switched the stereo off.

She smiled, went to him.

They sat on the soft leather couch knee to knee, hand in hand. Touched glasses.

Sipped, eye-smiling at each other. Put the glasses down on lucite blocks.

He took both her hands, looked into her eyes. "The first thing," he said, "is I love you." He leaned, kissed her lips meeting his. "That's why I'm telling you this. Remember that, please. You're going to get angry, very. I promise. So remember, I'm telling you because I love you. You once said I could tell you anything; I'm taking you at your word."

"If you have a wife and children," she said, "I'm going to cream you. I mean it."

"No, no," he said, shaking his head. "No . . ." He drew a breath, looked down.

She watched him.

"The second thing," he said, "is I've told you a lot of lies." He raised his head, looked at her. "Nothing *but* lies, practically."

She said, "Such as . . ."

He drew breath. "I'm not a computer programmer," he said. "Professionally I mean. I can write programs—I wrote the games, back when I was in high school—but those were lies about free-lancing, and Price Waterhouse and ABC."

"You don't own the building," she said.

"No I do," he said. "That was one of the true things, everything about my family, and the money . . . Kay, listen—" His blue eyes sparked, his hands gripped hers. "Suppose I told you I was dealing drugs—I'm not, but suppose that's what I told you. What would you say? Really. If I told you that."

She looked at him.

"What would you say?" he asked. "This is just what-if. Honestly."

She said, "I'd say 'Quit this minute. It's wrong, it's criminal, it's crazy. Thank your lucky stars you haven't been caught.' "

"And suppose I did. Quit. What then?"

"What do you mean, what then?"

He said, "What would you *do* if I *quit*?"

She drew breath. "I would try to help you find a legal occupation," she said. "I would try to understand, and help *you* understand, why you had done such a stupid, risky thing. And help you—not get into it again."

"Would you blow the whistle on me?" he asked.

"Of course not," she said. "Don't be silly. I love you too, remember?"

He nodded. Leaned, kissed her lips.

She drew back, freed her hands. "Pete, darling, please," she said, "get to the point; I don't know *what* the hell to expect."

"We're at it," he said.

He picked up a remote controller, thumbed red lights onto the TV and the VCR beside it.

"Show and tell?" she said.

"You got it," he said.

The TV screen came alight—a golf ball rolling across green turf. It plunked in the cup, applause rippled. The screen went dark, another red gleam on the VCR.

She picked up her glass. Said, "I wish you would—" A living room appeared in black and white, viewed from above, a man walking around gathering papers that rustled, plates that clinked.

She put the glass down. Watched.

Him.

In that room. Taking empty glasses off the lucite blocks. He raised his face, smiled at her. "Hi, Kay," he said. Kissed at her.

She turned to him beside her, blue eyes watching her. "Hi, Kay," he said. Kissed at her.

She turned, looked up at the chrome-centered Art Deco light. At him. "I don't *get* it," she said.

"There's a camera up between the floors," he said, pointing the controller aside; the TV clicked off. "And a glass thread coming down through the stem of the light."

She squinted at him. "*Why?*" she asked. "Are you with the CIA? Or the FBI?"

"No," he said, "but it's stuff they use. Takai, Japanese, the best in the world. A former colonel in the CIA helped me set up the system, procured everything. . . ."

She looked at him. Said, "The 'system'?"

He nodded. "That's what it is, Kay," he said. "A whole system. *All* the lights feed into cameras. Yours included."

She looked at him.

"I've been watching you since the day you moved in," he said. "And listening. To your phone conversations too. Both ends. That's how I was so *intuitive* and *perceptive*."

She stared at him.

"I told you you would get angry," he said. "I violated your privacy and in a sense it's almost as if I raped you. But if I hadn't, would we be here now? Would we have had the wonderful times we've had? And don't I really know you anyway, more sides of you than anyone else does? Even if I pirated some of the data?"

She stared at him.

"I was going to let the relationship just tail off," he said, "but I can't. It's too important to me, I love you too much. And having to lie all the time spoils it, not being able to share things . . ." He shrugged, smiled. "So . . . I'm in your hands now, because you could blow the whistle and get me into a lot of very hot water."

She stared at him.

Looked away. At her glass. Picked it up, her hand quivering.

Sipped, ice in the glass tinkling.

He watched her, reaching aside, putting the remote controller down.

She swallowed. Put the glass down. Looked at him. Said, "You watch everybody?"

He nodded.

"Guided by the light?" she said. "Searching for tomorrow?"

Pink-cheeked, he nodded. Smiled. "God, you're quick," he said. "It took me years to see that. Sure, that's how it *started*, but it's a whole other thing now, far beyond that."

She shook her head. "I don't understand—" She looked at the blank TV. "*How?* How do you—" She turned her hands out.

He stood up. "Come on, I'll show you," he said. "It's next door." He bent and picked his glass up, drank.

"Next door?" she said.

He put the glass down, backhanded his mouth. "I have thirteen B too," he said. "The Johnsons are another lie." He moved away, waited.

She looked at him.

Got up, putting a hand to the back of the couch.

Followed him out of the apartment.

Across the hallway.

He unlocked 13B's door, braced it open for her. "If you think it was messy in there," he said, "you ought to see what it looked like in here."

THE KITCHEN WAS the kitchen, half-lit in the hallway's light and a green glow from the pass-through.

The foyer was pallid green. A green-shaded lamp in the living room hung before a colossal wall-to-wall sea monster, all gray-green scales, lying on a curved sweep of tan.

Television screens, a curving multitiered wall of them, two mammoth ones in the center. A hundred or more dark screens, each with a green glint moving sideways as she moved nearer, the light growing brighter.

He was playing the dimmer behind her.

Ranks of buttons and switches on the curved tan console.

A black posture-back armchair before it.

She stopped a few feet back. Stood scanning the half-dozen rows of screens, the pale digits above—*4A, 5A, 6A*—and across the middle—*6B, 7B, 8B* . . .

He went to the console's left end, turning; stood with a hand on its rounded rim, watching her. "Three for each apartment," he said, "except this one. The security cameras too—the lobby, the elevators, et cetera. A hundred and thirty altogether. I can feed them onto either of the masters. The distortion is electronically corrected; what's left I don't even notice. The eye adjusts pretty quickly."

She turned her head, looked at him. "*Three?*" she said.

He nodded. "I said, all the lights."

She stared at him.

"I know, it's a little gross," he said. "I was ten or eleven when I first got the idea, just a thing I used to fantasize about. Then, watching them start this building, when I saw I could actually do it, I never thought of *not* including the bathrooms." He smiled. "They were crucial originally. And a lot of good conversations take place there."

She looked at him, drew a breath. "You have *got* to realize," she said, "that this is the most—the most *monstrous, horrendous* invasion of privacy that could possibly be perpetrated! Not just against *me*"—she clasped herself with both hands, leaning toward him—"although Jesus God, to say you love someone and all the time be—my *God*, I can't even—"

"I do love you," he said, moving toward her.

"Against *everybody*!" she said. "How can you *do* this to people? It's appalling!" She looked at the screens. "My *God* . . ."

"They don't *know*," he said.

"That doesn't matter!" she cried.

"It does," he said, close to her. "Did it *hurt* you that I was watching?"

"It hurts me *now*!"

"Because now you *know*! Look"—he took her by the shoulders—"let's not argue about it, I expected you to feel this way. I'm closing it down." He held her, looking at her. "If I have to choose between it and you," he said, "I choose you. I'm *quitting*. It's finished. No more."

They looked at each other.

"You'd better," she said. "This must be against a dozen laws. And you'll be sued penniless if the other tenants find out, no matter *how* much money you have."

"That's what I meant about hot water," he said. Breathed a sigh, looking at her. "I'm sorry I hurt you," he said. "I never saw you do anything that wasn't beautiful, or heard you say anything dumb."

"Did you see Hubert Sheer fall?" she asked.

"No, I didn't," he said. "And I didn't see him afterwards. You can't see into the showers, the angle is wrong. There's glare on the door and all the black makes it worse. Look." He let go of her, turned, leaned over the chairback. "No," she said.

Reaching to the console, he looked back at her, his head brushing the green shade. "*My* bathroom," he said, "not that one."

She said, "I'll take your word."

He stood and turned, faced her. "I hardly watched him at all," he said, the green glints stirring on the screens. "He was usually reading. I thought he'd gone on the trip he was talking about and left the lights on by mistake. That happens." He drew a breath. "The only death I saw," he said, "was Billy Webber when he OD'd. There were two girls with him, which was why I was watching, and they called an ambulance the minute he started convulsing. I wasn't home when Brendan Connahay and Naomi Singer died, and there's no camera where Rafael, the super before Dmitri, had the accident."

She said, "Do you watch Sam too?"

"Yes," he said. "He doesn't know. Look, I happen to have done a lot of good here, and not just for him. I help people out, financially and in other ways too, sometimes through the foundation, sometimes just cash in the mail. *Families* of people. Maggie Hoffman's niece needed a liver transplant, in Shreveport. The mother's a wonderful woman, gutsy, single, broke; I sent the money. The week before last. The Kestenbaums, who were in your apartment; I helped them too."

She shook her head. "It's wrong," she said. Looked at him. "It's wrong."

"So I'm closing it down," he said. He took her at the waist with both hands, smiled at her. "Mommy says no and I'm a good boy, right?" He kissed her cheek. "I can't junk it," he said, "because it would be a little hard explaining where everything's coming from, but what we'll do is get a locksmith up here and change the lock, and you'll keep the keys. There's a door in back too, through the closets; I mention it as a sign of good faith; you never would have noticed it. You can put a combination lock on that. And that's it. I'll do some programming, or maybe finish my degree."

She looked at him.

"Is it worse than dealing drugs?" he asked.

"Do you really mean that?" she asked.

"About the locks? Yes," he said. "I told you, I choose *you*."

They looked at each other. Hugged each other, kissed.

She hugged him tight; sighed and shook her head, looking over his shoulder at the screens. "Dr. Palme *too*?" she asked.

"Yes," he said. "See what I meant about having to lie all the time?"

"Jesus . . ." She looked at the green-glinting screens. "That's the *pits*," she said, "watching people in therapy . . ."

"They *don't know*," he said.

She looked at the screens. Drew back, peered at him. Said, "And this is what you've been *doing* for three years?"

"It's the most fascinating thing you've ever seen, Kay," he said. "Dramatic, funny, heart-breaking, sexy, suspenseful, educational . . ."

She touched his cheek, shaking her head. "Living soaps," she said.

"No, *life*," he said. "The real thing, the soap that God watches. A sliver of it anyway. No actresses, no actors, no directors. No writers or editors. No commercials. And every bit of it true, not somebody's version of the truth—like all the *books* you've read."

She drew from his arms. "You son of a bitch," she said, "you're trying to sell me on it. . . ."

"Just watch for an hour," he said, reaching to her. She pushed his hand away, heading for the foyer. "Tomorrow the locksmith," she said.

"*Tomorrow?*" he said, going after her.

"Tomorrow," she said, opening the door. "They work Sundays." She went out into the hallway. "Jesus," she said.

Leaned to the mirror, poked her hair.

He came out, closed the door, tried it.

"You're too much," she said. "Mr. Open, Mr. I'm-In-Your-Hands-Now—pushing his peeping machine. When I think of the *conversations* you listened to, never mind the goddamn *bathroom* . . ."

"I apologized," he said. "What do you want me to do, grovel? I have something terrific I want to show you."

"You've shown it," she said, plucking at the pullover's collar. "God almighty, what did you *spend* on that?"

"Counting the bribes," he said, "not counting the building, a little over six million."

She looked at him in the mirror. "That's a genuine sin," she said.

"The building's gone up ten mill," he said. "I'm ahead on the deal."

"That's worse," she said. "But it makes me feel fine about locking it up." She turned, stepped to the elevators, touched between them, looked at him. "I don't want you watching me tonight," she said.

"I won't," he said. Raised his hand.

"Or anyone else," she said.

"Oh come on," he said. "The last night? And a *Saturday* night?"

They looked at each other.

"On second thought," she said, "maybe *I'd* better watch *you.* Go turn off the lights. You're staying at my place."

He went to 13A, smiling.

"Don't look so smug," she said. "I'm really pissed off at you."

■　　■　　■

"LEGALLY IT'S STILL a gray area," he said, lying spooned behind her, clasping her breasts, his cheek in her hair. "Especially when the camera is outside the rented premises, which it is in this case. I'm very well informed on privacy issues; the couple in ten B are with the ACLU."

"Jesus Christmas," she said, "you spy on the *ACLU*?"

"That's why I approved them," he said. "I figured they'd keep me up to date. Actually they turned out to be kind of astounding for lawyers."

"Good night, Pete," she said.

"Good night, Kay." He kissed her neck, squeezed her breasts.

They snuggled closer, lay silent.

Felice turned around against their blanketed feet.

"Incidentally," he said, "this was the third apartment house the Colonel worked on. And he did a hotel too."

They lay silent.

"Here in New York?" she asked.

"He wouldn't talk about them."

"Gee, I'm glad he's so ethical."

"Except he said the hotel's system is computerized; it only shows the rooms where there's movement. It can even discriminate between one person and two. This is small potatoes here."

"Small immoral ones."

They lay silent.

"Come on . . ." he said. "Half an hour and then we'll call the locksmith. No bathrooms. No Sam if that's a problem."

"Good *night*, Peter," she said.

They lay silent.

"It's not just watching," he said. "It's putting different things alongside each other, or the audio from one apartment over the video from another. You get all kinds of—contrasts and harmonies. Sometimes it's like playing an organ. A people organ."

"Will you shut up and go to sleep?"

"Good night," he said. Kissed her neck.

They lay silent.

A blow shook the ceiling.

"Jesus," she said, "what do they *do* up there?"

"None of your business," he said.

"Oh, fuck you . . ."

He kissed her neck.

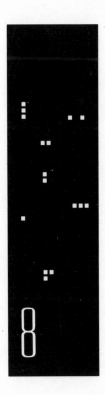

8

Half an hour," she said.

He unlocked 13B's door, and reaching in, switched on the foyer light. "I hope there's something good," he said, bracing the door open for her. "It's liable to be just a few Jets fans."

"I thought it was supposed to be continuous fascination," she said, going in.

"Beautiful Sunday afternoons aren't prime time. And it's Thanksgiving weekend, don't forget. A lot of people went home."

She stood at the rim of the living room's darkness, her hand going where her switch upstairs was. She pressed, and turned the green-shaded lamp up full, lighting the tan console, the gray screens.

"I'll get a chair. . . ."

She stood surveying the wall-to-wall curve of green-glinting screens, six rows high from the console to near the ceiling, single rows passing over and under the mammoth center screens; six rows high on either side, pale digits glowing across the top and midline—2 through 11 on the left, 12 through 21 on the right, A's above, B's below.

She walked nearer, slipping her hands into her jeans pockets.

Stood behind the posture-back armchair looking at the console's regiments of paired toggle switches and push buttons, patterned and plastic-labeled to match the screens. A center bank of knobs and larger switches; farther back, sunk in tan laminate, two VCR's.

An inset face-up clock—blue digits, 12:55—a phone, a pad in a clipboard. A bowl of jelly beans. Luscious colors.

The door closed behind her.

She watched his pearly reflection in 1 and 2, the center screens, coming in behind a tall white chair, bringing it to her left. "Did you tape *me*?" she asked, turning.

He put down one of his white leather dining chairs; held its peaked back, looking at her. "Yes," he said. "The night you moved in, in the tub, but it's so dark you can hardly see anything. And the two of us, that first Saturday night."

She looked away. "I don't believe it," she said.

"I set it when I came down for the champagne," he said. Smiled at her. "Just in case. You don't want to miss a major event. Don't make me erase it; it's super-safe and think what fun it'll be when we're old. We'll probably be the only couple in the world with a tape of their first time together."

She looked at him. Drew a breath. "I wouldn't doubt it," she said. Turned and sat.

He squared the chair toward the screens, bent over it, kissed her head.

He went and dimmed the green-shaded lamp; watched it, dimming it low. "I've got soda and stuff here," he said. "Do you want anything?"

She shook her head, looking down, rubbing at the back of a hand.

He came and sat in his chair, rolled close to the console. Switched on a red gleam, a hum from the back of the apartment.

She sat straight in the straight-backed chair, crossed her legs, folded her arms.

"This'll take a second," he said. "I'm cutting out the bathrooms and Sam's apartment."

In the pallid light she watched his hand riding on its shadow, clicking along the row of toggles nearest her. "What's the humming?" she asked.

"The power supply." His hand clicked back along a farther row of toggles. "The voltage has to be stepped down and converted, from AC to DC. There'd be too much heat and noise in here with a separate transformer for each screen. I've got a big one in back wired right into the mains." He clicked at the right-hand switches. "I'll close the door if it bothers you."

"It's all right," she said. Looked at his turned head. "It would really be super," she said, "if you put this much effort and industry into something worthwhile."

"Give me time," he said. "I've got other projects in mind. Okay . . ."—he faced front, clicked switches—"welcome to the *real* Golden Age of Television . . ."

The screens bloomed blue-white in rows of rooms on both sides. The third row down stayed dark, and the bottom row except the screens under the large ones—the building's entrance, the lobby, the mailroom, both elevators. "Let's check out Felice," he said, touching buttons. The center screens ballooned with all-around overviews of her living room, her bedroom.

"Good Lord," she said.

He touched knobs on the console.

She looked at her furniture, her patterned rugs, her *Times* scattered around the bedroom, her books, her plants, her ornaments.

"You'll get used to the perspective," he said. "Here she is. Hi, Felice."

Felice walked past the bed on the right-hand screen, newspaper rustling under her. She walked to the window at the top of the screen, hopped to the sill. Lay down in the sunlight, lifted a hind leg, licked it.

She smiled in the blue-white light.

"Oh shit, I forgot," he said, "we should have waited till three. Ruby's having a séance and it'll be interesting. Ruby Clupeida, with the perfume." He touched a button before her, one before him. "She's into spiritualism." On the left-hand screen, Giorgio, in a dark caftan, brought a chair to a round table. "There's a psychic who's been ripping her off for months," he said. "I've seen him checking his notes in the bathroom. And she's finally gotten suspicious and has an expert coming. He's going to pretend to be her father's business partner. The father is dead and has been *communicating*."

"That's beautiful furniture," she said. "Jacobean."

"Family heirlooms," he said. "Her mother is suing her over them. She claims Ruby took them without permission."

"I gather she's not a man in drag."

"No." He smiled, scanning the monitors. "That was funny, when you said she looked like one, because you had just asked me about Vida, who is, more or less."

"*What?*"

"He's a pre-op transsexual," he said. "He had the hormone treatments but when it came to the actual operation he had second thoughts. He's been fighting with his lover about it for almost a year. And you'll never guess—oh good, Jay and Lisa are here." He touched buttons. "The Fishers, four A. She's been having an affair with her boss and her sister tipped him off last week. She's been denying it." In a high-tech living room on the right-hand screen, an attractive dark-haired woman she'd seen in the elevator stood in pajamas looking out the window. A man in pajamas crouched at the TV, adjusting it. "It's beautiful out," Lisa Fisher said.

"Go for a walk," Jay Fisher said. "Call Ben, it's okay with me."

"Oh God," Lisa Fisher said, "if you're going to start in again . . ."

On the left-hand screen, the goateed man on twelve sat down at a desk in a half-furnished living room and picked up the phone. "David Hoenenkamp," Pete said while the Fishers argued. "An ex-priest, now in advertising. He has his own agency, small but successful. He's separated from the woman he left the church for."

They listened to David Hoenenkamp explaining to a client why he was resigning the account.

The Fishers arguing.

"Fantastic clarity, isn't it?" he said, offering the jelly beans.

She nodded, taking a couple.

"Takai," he said. "Japanese, the best in the world." He put the bowl down on the blue 1:07, took a few beans himself.

They watched the Sweringens on 1, the Fishers on 2. He switched the sound back and forth.

"I ASSURE YOU it's not a question of money," Stefan said on 1, going into the kitchen, "it's the time involved. Do you realize how long it takes to find the parts?"

"Hey, what time is it?" she asked.

He moved the bowl—from 3:02. "Jeez," he said.

"Good grief," she said.

He killed the sound. Swiveled to her.

They looked at each other.

"And this was *nothing*, Kay," he said. "Almost nobody here. No Dr. Palme. No sex even, for God's sake."

She said, "I didn't expect it to be boring."

"You ought to see it in a few hours," he said, "when every-body's getting home."

She shifted around, leaned to him, took his hands in hers. "Petey, it's *wrong*," she said, "no matter *how* interesting and—affecting it is. And you *know* it means big trouble if anyone finds out. It could ruin your whole life. *Our* whole lives . . ."

They looked at each other.

She said, "It's something you have to put behind you. Not just for *us*. For your own sake."

He sighed, nodded. "I guess . . ." he said.

She let go his hands.

He swiveled, opened a drawer, brought out the Yellow Pages. Opened the thick book in his lap, swiveling back. Sighed, looked at her.

She looked at him.

He riffled pages in the blue-white light, found the locksmiths. "Wow, look how many," he said, turning pages.

"How are you going to work this?" she asked. "Will Terry let a locksmith up here with no Johnsons around?"

He looked at her.

"And if you call someone to thirteen A," she said, "will he change the lock here?"

He said, "I didn't think of that."

She said, "You goddamn liar . . ."

He raised his right hand. "Kay, I swear I didn't. I was so anxious to get you to watch for a while . . ." He leaned to her. "Look," he said, "it really doesn't make any *difference*. All we have to do is fix this door so it can't be opened from outside, nail a piece of wood to the floor or something, and you can still put a lock on the door in back. Same effect." He smiled at her. "We can play games where I try to get you to tell the combination. If I succeed, you change it."

She sat a moment, looking at him. Shook her head. "No," she said. "I've changed my mind. I'm not going to be Mommy-taking-care-of-you all the time. That's not the kind of relation-ship I want. You're an adult, Pete. You're going to have to be responsible for your own actions. You know how I feel about this. If you really want an ongoing relationship, you're going to have to do the locking up yourself."

He sighed. "The honor system?" he said.

"Yes," she said.

He nodded, closed the phone book, swiveled, put it on the console. "You're right, of course." He swiveled back, smiling at her. "You're really going to shape me up. . . ." He took her hands, bent, kissed them. Sat looking at her, his eyes a deeper blue in the blue-white. "I will," he said. "I'm going to get onto those other projects. Actually I've sort of started on one. There are some things going on here that I'm very involved in—a couple of Dr. Palme's patients, and eleven B, the two women there, and the Ostrows right above you—so I can't swear I'm going to quit cold turkey, but I'm going to cut way down and taper off fast. I promise I will."

"I hope so, Pete," she said. "I really do."

They leaned to each other, kissed.

"And I won't watch *you* any more, ever," he said, freeing a hand, turning. He clicked switches. The 20B monitors went dark, the next to the last in the lower right rows. He smiled at her. "You and Sam," he said. "Symmetrical."

She looked around at the dark second screens in the lower left rows. Noticed, turning back, new movement in 8B.

"That's the psychic," he said. Touched buttons.

Hand in hand they looked at the masters. Ruby and another woman ushered a stout dark-suited man into the living room. Jay got into an overcoat, shouting at Lisa who was talking on the phone with a finger in her ear.

"Turn the sound on," Kay said. "Just for a minute."

■   ■   ■

FIRST THING MONDAY morning she called the legal department. Wayne was there. She asked how Sandy and the kids were. They were fine. "I need some information about the laws concerning invasion of privacy," she said. "Specifically, a situation where someone bugs an apartment with a videocamera and rents it out, on a standard lease, here in New York."

"The tenant being unaware of the videocamera."

"Yes," she said. "The phone is tapped too. I've got a manuscript based on that situation, and according to the author it's a gray area legally. Is he right, and if so, exactly how gray?"

"I couldn't say offhand, that's not my bailiwick, but I'll be glad to run it down for you. I *can* tell you that a phone tap, if it's unauthorized, is a federal offense."

"I thought as much," she said.

"Probably state as well. I'll get back to you about the videocamera. It shouldn't take long."

"It's outside the apartment," she said. "He says that's a factor. There's a glass thread coming in through the ceiling light."

"Is it being done for a business-related purpose?"

"No," she said, "it's just a matter of watching."

"Aha. And the heroine moves in."

"How did you guess?" she said.

She asked Sara to get Florence Leary Winthrop and to hold all calls except Wayne.

Half an hour later she put Florence on hold. "Wayne?"

"Yes. Your writer's right. There's no federal or state criminal law yet against visual electronic surveillance per se. The landlord could be subject to a civil suit if the tenant found out, but the only criminal charge he might face, other than the unauthorized phone tapping—which is a five-year felony, by the way—would be running afoul of the state law against peeping, a very minor charge. And even that would be open to challenge."

"I'm surprised," she said.

"So am I. There may be some legislation pending. Your best bet for information on that would probably be the ACLU."

She thanked him; apologized to Florence.

"I told you," Pete said that evening, smiling. "They're very knowledgeable and they never stop yakking. Two lawyers."

"The penalty for unauthorized phone tapping," she said, "is five years."

"I know that," he said.

They were in Table d'Hôte, a small storefront restaurant on Ninety-second Street. Couples and foursomes were at all but one of the eight antique tables; the noise level of conversation and cutlery was high. They were in a corner at a round table, sitting knee against knee, sipping white wine, buttering pieces of marbled bread.

"I can't *un*tap them at this point," he said, "not without breaking through the basement ceiling. But nobody'll ever find out. And I'm really tapering off. I didn't watch at all today, not that Mondays are fantastic. During the day, I mean. Monday nights are. Everybody's home."

"What did you do?" she asked.

"Some computer work on the project," he said. "And I'll tell you right now, it's something I'd rather not talk about until certain details have been ironed out. I know you'll understand that."

"Of course," she said. "I wasn't probing. I was just curious about how you spent the day. It must have been hard not to watch. I couldn't stop thinking about it, how hypnotic it is."

"Because it's real," he said. "It's like the difference between seeing cars piling up in a movie and a real accident in the street."

"And never knowing what's coming next," she said.

"Sure, that's a big part of it," he said. "The total unpredictability, and the variety."

She sighed, sipped her wine. "I wish to hell it weren't so wrong," she said.

"It's *considered* wrong," he said, "but nobody gets hurt and I'll bet there isn't anyone who wouldn't want to watch for a while."

She looked at him. "No more," she said.

"I know," he said. "I told you, I didn't at all today, and one of Dr. Palme's most interesting patients is on Monday."

The waiter set handsomely garnished Victorian plates before them—grilled swordfish, poached salmon.

Delicious. They traded tastes.

He told her about some of Dr. Palme's patients.

The tall couple on seventeen came in from the street; one of the waiters greeted them, pointed them to the vacant table two away from theirs.

"The Coles in seventeen A," he murmured. "The building's leading kinks."

"We're not?" she said.

"*Us?* No way. We're fifth or sixth."

"And climbing."

On the way home they stopped at the flower-banked Korean grocery on the corner, picked up orange juice and apples for her, milk and grapes and coffee for him. He put change in the paper cup of the ragged man outside.

They crossed Ninety-second Street, waited for the sign to change. Looked up at the towering pink-lit building, its twin lanes of windows glowing, glinting to its dark top. "It's an odd feeling," she said, hugging his arm, looking up, "knowing the people behind the windows . . ."

"I thought that was how it was back home," he said, watching her, smiling.

"Oh sure, exactly the same . . ."

They smiled at each other. Puckered, kissed.

Crossed the avenue.

Walt, in winter maroon, backed the door open as they came near.

"Hi, Walt," they said.

"Miss Norris, Mr. Henderson . . ."

Crossing the lobby, he said in her ear, "He's having an affair with Denise Smith in five B."

"He *is?*"

"He makes out a lot." He touched the up button; they watched Walt outside, opening a cab door. "It's the voice that gets them," he said. "He used to sing at the City Opera, in the chorus. He and Ruby had a thing going last year but he broke it off. She had him walking Ginger all the time."

The black/white couple came in with Christmas shopping bags from Lord & Taylor. Everybody nodded, smiled.

Pete said, " 'Tis the season."

"Yes, it is," the man said, smiling.

The number-one elevator came.

They rode up in silence.

After the door closed on seven, he said, "Bill and Carol Wagnall. *Very* interesting."

"I'm sure," she said.

They got out at thirteen to drop off his groceries.

"Just a little?" he said.

"Pete," she said, "you know what'll happen. . . ."

They looked at each other.

She said, "I don't deny I'd *like* to. . . ."

"They *don't know*," he said.

She shook her head. "Jesus," she said.

"Come on," he said. "We'll set a reasonable time and we'll really stick to it. I said I wasn't going to quit cold turkey, didn't I? One hour. But really. We'll set the alarm."

She sighed. "All right," she said. "But *really*. One hour."

They set the alarm.

THEY WORKED UP a sweat at the Vertical Club, battling the biceps machines side by side. Swam laps in the pool.

Went with Roxie and Fletcher to an Off Broadway hit. Didn't think much of it, though Roxie and Fletcher enjoyed it. Roxie invited them up for a nightcap; they passed.

A five-year-old could have worked it. You touched the 10A top button, then the 1 button in the center bank—and presto, there was the 10A living room on 1. Anne Stangerson holding her ears, refusing to listen to an old woman reading from a sheet of paper—her mother reading her living will.

They watched a few minutes, while on 2, the Gruens in 14B, naked on their bed with a book and a calculator, worked out the best time to get Daisy pregnant.

She took the left-hand monitors and 1, he took the right-hand monitors and 2. They found contrasts and harmonies.

Played duets on the people organ.

She stood leaning by her office window with her arms folded, looking down at the shiny necklace of rainswept traffic far below. She sighed, looked ahead. A woman at a window across the street looked away. "Kay," Sara said, "is anything wrong?"

She turned, smiling. "Just the usual," she said. "Homelessness, drug-related crime, the national debt . . ."

She came down on an at-home day to have a look at Dr. Palme. Two black posture-back chairs stood before the console.

"What do you know," Pete said, "it divided."

They watched Dr. Palme and Nina.

And Dick.

And Joanna.

DIADEM HAD TAKEN a table at a black-tie dinner dance for the Literacy Volunteers of America, in the Celeste Bartos Forum of the Forty-second Street Library. In the cab on the way down Fifth Avenue, in faux fur and beaded burgundy velvet, she said, "Really, be prepared for dirty looks, maybe remarks too. I've seen it before. Older men get nasty, especially when the woman's not deformed. It's an animal thing, the stags bumping antlers."

"Will you stop worrying?" he said. "Older women and younger men are all over the place. Look at Babette and Allan."

"That's five years, for God's sake," she said.

"Relax," he said. "Everybody's going to be nice. I'll bet you a massage."

She turned to the window. "You're on. . . ."

Traffic crept—the tree in Rockefeller Center.

Which was breathtaking, though, as they inched past it, the dazzle of lights at the end of the plaza, the lines of gauze angels lifting gilt trumpets . . .

In the hall outside the forum, she took him by the hand—"Here we go"—and brought him to a gray-haired couple at the end of one of the coat-check lines. "Hi!" she said. "This is Peter Henderson! Pete, June del Vecchio, Norman del Vecchio."

"Hello!" June said, shaking Pete's hand, smiling at him.

"Hello," Norman said, shaking Pete's hand. Smiling at him.

"It's a pleasure to meet you," he said to them. "Kay told me you're active in Civitas. My father was too; I wonder if you knew him. John Henderson?"

Norman said, "Of U.S. Steel?"

"Yes," he said.

"We did, *yes*," Norman said, smiling at him.

"What a charmer he was!" June said. "You have his eyes, and his smile!"

"And what a salesman!" Norman said. "He got us money from builders we'd fought against!"

"You'd better watch out, Kay," June said, "if Peter's cut from the same cloth!"

She smiled. "Thanks for the warning," she said.

"What field are you in, Peter?" Norman asked.

"I've been doing some computer programming," he said. "At the moment I'm sort of in flux."

"Maybe you could have a look at our billing system; God knows it could use overhauling. Oh Jim, come say hello to Peter Henderson, the son of an old friend. . . ."

There were cocktails first in Astor Hall. Everybody was nice.

Stuart had gotten to Sam's material and thanked her for it. "It's the kind of stuff I love," he said. "He's coming in next week. If we hit it off, I'm going to offer him a small advance."

"Oh good, I'm glad," she said.

"That's great," Pete said.

"Do you know him too, Pete?" Stuart asked.

"Just to say hello to in the elevator," he said. "We're all in the same building."

Wendy, smiling, said, "Would you perchance be the mysterious owner?"

"No," he said, smiling at Kay, "we haven't figured out yet who it is. The leading candidates are a pair of lawyers."

The forum's glass dome—ribbed with steel, rimmed with bulbs, a spaceship out of H. G. Wells—was lighted from above with pink shading into violet. The tables beneath it were purple and violet with white-and-gold settings, pink-and-violet floral arrangements, tall pink candles. A four-piece combo played Sondheim and Porter.

The conversation at the Diadem table was about the traffic and the city's crumbling infrastructure, Japanese investment strategies, health food, living wills.

After the Cornish game hen, Norman said, "Kay?" She smiled at Pete as she followed Norman onto the dance floor. They said some hellos; danced to "Let's Do It" with air between them.

"He's unusually perceptive," Norman said. "Well informed too."

"Isn't he?" she said.

"I hope he's more stable emotionally than his father. Married four times, I believe. Always actresses. I wonder if . . ."

They danced, couples close around them.

"What?" she asked.

"One of them died in a fall," Norman said. "Down the stairs of their duplex. I wonder if that was Peter's mother."

"It was," she said. "Thea Marshall."

"A curving marble staircase, according to the story."

"The story?" She smiled at Pete, winking at her over June's gray curls a few couples away.

"Hello there," Norman said to someone. "Oh, a bit of gossip that went around at the time—what was it, twelve or thirteen years ago? There was a party in progress when it happened. She had suitcases with her, that's why she lost her footing. She was rushing to catch a plane—going home for Christmas, a last-minute impulse. That's what Henderson said afterwards. She was from someplace in Canada. Well, supposedly one of the suitcases popped a latch when it hit bottom and someone saw bathing suits and summer dresses."

"Do you think we can make a deal?" Pete asked, June smiling on his arm alongside them.

"Oh yes, indeed," Norman said, letting go of her, taking June. "An eminently fair deal all around." Pete slipped an arm around her waist, smiling at her. June said, "Aren't we gallant this evening," as Norman danced her into the crowd.

"What about bathing suits and summer dresses?" Pete asked, drawing her close, taking her hand, turning her with the music. She looked at him—handsome in his black tie, his blue eyes smiling at her. He said, "That's what it sounded like."

She said, "I don't know. I wasn't listening."

He held her tight, pressed his cheek to hers, turned her. "Who owes who a massage?" he asked.

They danced in the crowd of dancers, to "Easy to Love," under the steel-ribbed glass dome lit with violet shading into purple.

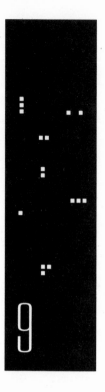

9

She had pictured it in some work-related limbo; how awful that it had happened in the apartment, at a time when more than likely he had been there to see it—before Christmas, a party going on.

She thought about it—again—watching Lisa packing a suit-case on 1 and Maggie, poor Maggie, unpacking a suitcase on 2. He was over in 13A waiting to pay the man from Jolly Chan's, coming up in the number-one elevator along with Phil and the McAuliffs.

The bathing suits and summer dresses, if they'd been real and not a mistake on someone's part, suggested California.

Which suggested Sam.

Which suggested an assist down the stairs by John Henderson.

She had edited dozens of Gothics and thrillers, she reminded herself. Fatal falls in real life were accidents more often than not. Even down curving marble staircases.

They'd had a place in Palm Beach; maybe that was where Thea had been going, and John had said she'd been going home only because it sounded like a better reason for parting at Christmas.

Though surely Thea had had bathing suits and summer dresses in Palm Beach. . . .

The door opened; she swiveled in her chair. Watched Pete come into the foyer with a brown paper shopping bag. He smiled—John Henderson's smile. John's son. "What do you want first?" he asked, closing the door.

"Whatever, darling," she said. Smiled at him.

He smiled in the pale blue-white, looking beyond her. "Nice," he said. "*A Tale of Two Suitcases.* Did I say she'd be back?" He went into the kitchen. Light flooded from the pass-through.

She swiveled. Watched Lisa trying to close her suitcase, Maggie putting hers in the closet.

She swiveled, got up, went to the kitchen. He turned from unloading the bag onto the counter. "I'll do it, honey," he said.

"I want to move around a little," she said. Took plates from the dish rack, put them on the counter by him. "Mmm, smells good," she said.

"Why don't they mark these things . . ." He lifted along the metal rim of a circular container.

She took forks and soup spoons from the drawer, put the spoons by him. "The suitcases reminded me," she said, "Norman told me about your mother's fall."

He turned and looked at her. "Was he there?" he asked.

"No," she said, "he heard about it. I knew that was how she

died, Sam told me, but I didn't know it was at home." She touched his arm, looking at him. "Were you there?" she asked.

He nodded. "She'd just said good-bye to me," he said. "About two minutes before."

She winced, squeezed his arm.

"I didn't see it happen," he said. "I was in my room." He smiled. "Watching *Charlie's Angels*." The smile went. "All of a sudden it got quiet downstairs. There were a lot of people there, thirty or forty, and it got real quiet. . . ." He drew a breath and looked to the container, lifted along its rim with both thumbs. "I think this is the curried shrimp," he said.

She stood close beside him, holding his arm, watching his hands. "Where was she going?" she asked.

"To my grandparents'," he said. "In Nova Scotia. Have you ever been there?"

"No," she said.

"Neither have I," he said. "She made it sound pretty grim. They visited us a few times, we didn't go there."

She kissed his ear, let go his arm, took a pinch of napkins from the box while he spooned shrimp and rice onto the plates. "What would you like to drink?" she asked.

He squinted, pursed his lips. "Beer," he said.

"Good idea," she said, putting the forks and napkins on the tray. She went to the refrigerator, opened it. "What did your father die of?" she asked.

"Bone marrow cancer," he said. "When did Norman tell you? The other night?"

She got out two cans of beer, elbowed the door closed. "No," she said. "Yesterday, in the office. He's impressed as all get-out with you, you know that?"

"Come on," he said, "he's impressed with my money."

"Both," she said.

She got glasses and brought everything in on the tray. He brought in the two filled plates.

It was Saturday night. They watched till after two.

"Some night," she said, turning around on his lap and hugging him. He swiveled his chair while they kissed, swiveled full circle, twice. "Your average Saturday," he said.

She got up and stretched, yawning. He caressed her back, turned, opened a drawer. "I'm going to tape the Steins," he said, "just in case Springsteen shows up."

"He isn't going to," she said, buttoning her shirt. "Mark's full of shit, can't you tell?"

"Vladimir Horowitz was there once," he said, peeling plastic from a videocassette. "I've got it. Lesley did all the talking though."

"Do you tape much?" she asked, gathering plates and napkins from the console.

"No," he said, crumpling the plastic, drawing the cassette from the slipcase. "I did the first year or so—those two drawers are full—but there was always so much new stuff going on that I never got around to watching." He put the cassette into the right-hand VCR, homed it. "Now I only bother when there's a major event." He pressed buttons.

"Like us," she said, using a wadded napkin to brush bits of rice and chocolate cake from the console onto the plates.

"Right," he said, smiling. "And Springsteen *maybe*."

He shut down everything except the VCR and the input from the Steins' living room.

They straightened up in the kitchen. He took out the garbage when they left.

SHE HADN'T DONE more than glance at two of the manuscripts up for discussion Wednesday afternoon but she made it through the conference handily. Had in fact been more cogent in her comments, she told herself riding down to the forty-eighth floor, for having seen the woods and *not* the trees.

Sam sat reading in the reception area, a coat on the couch beside him. He looked at her over half-glasses, smiled and got up—in brown corduroy, plaid shirt, black tie, his gray hair looking freshly cut. "Hello!" he said, taking the glasses off, putting a *Publishers Weekly* down.

"Hi, Sam!" she said, going to him. "Stuart told me you were coming in."

"Congratulate me," he rasped, shaking her hand, smiling. "I'm a Diadem author."

"Oh, that's great!" she said. "I do, congratulations!" She hugged him. "I congratulate *us* too," she said.

He grinned at her. Pale scars webbed his flushed cheek and skewed nose. "He's drawing up a contract," he said. "An advance now and another when I get to the halfway mark."

"I knew he would like it," she said.

"I wanted to thank you."

She took him into her office, had Sara bring two coffees. They sat by the window in catty-cornered armchairs.

He scanned the glass-walled offices across the street. "Voyeur's heaven," he said.

She smiled, stirred her cup.

He sipped from his. "Stuart couldn't be more simpatico," he said. "He grew up in the movie business."

"That's why I gave it to him," she said. "Partly—the other part being that he's a good editor with substantial clout here."

"I really am grateful to you," he said. "This has made a significant difference for me. I think in the long run it was a mistake taking the grant. From the foundation. You know." He sipped from the white cup with the blue three-jeweled crown on it. "You can get awfully lazy and self-indulgent," he said, "when the grocery money is coming in regardless. Now, aside from being into the writing, and feeling that I'm getting better at it, I'm teaching more than before too." He smiled at her. "I'm beginning to have visions of getting on the talk shows and winding up directing again."

She smiled. "That's great," she said. "I hope it comes to pass."

They sipped.

"We're aiming for next spring," he said. "I've got about eighty pages now."

She said, "Would you give me something in return?"

"Name it," he said, looking at her.

"An answer to a personal question," she said.

He smiled. "Why not? I'm being godawful frank in the book. Go ahead."

"When Thea Marshall died," she said, "was she on her way to you?"

He drew back, his dark-ringed eyes squinting at her. "What in God's name gave you *that* idea?"

"Or to work out there?"

"*No,*" he said. "Definitely not. I asked her just a few weeks before and the conversation ended with her hanging up on me." He sighed, studying his cup. "We were on-again-off-again for over twenty years," he said. "She was married for most of them, to a filthy-rich husband she wouldn't let go of. She was honest about it, at least. She grew up poor and was paranoid about dying that way. She felt there was a good chance of it with me, I was already drinking too much. Whereas her husband was the chairman of U.S. Steel and hardly drank at all. It hadn't been a bad career move either." He sat straighter, shook his head. "No, she wasn't a risk-taker," he said. "She was going home, that's what the papers said. She was from Nova Scotia. Her folks were fishermen." He sipped his coffee.

Watching him, she said, "There was a rumor at the time that she'd packed for warm weather."

He looked at her.

"One of her suitcases opened when she fell."

He said, "Where'd you hear that?"

"From someone in their circle, or close to it."

He lowered the cup, holding it with both hands. Put it down. Sat looking ahead.

"Son of a gun . . ." he said. Scratched his ear. Looked at her. "You know, it would fit," he said. "He put out a contract on me.

I thought he had found some of my letters, or maybe she told him about us at the end."

"A *contract?*" she said.

He nodded. "Someone I knew who had mob connections warned me about it. I didn't believe him. Then I got this." He pointed at his nose and cheek. "I decided it was a good time to do some traveling. That's why the career ended. Mainly." He gazed ahead. "Son of a gun," he said. "I thought he had overreacted, but if she was leaving him, coming to me . . ."

She watched him.

He looked at her, smiled. "I firmly believe that the rumor was true," he said. "Please don't tell me if you hear anything to the contrary."

She smiled. "Mum's the word," she said.

"Packed for warm weather . . ."

"Bathing suits and summer dresses."

"Now I owe you for two favors," he said.

She asked him where he had traveled; while they finished their coffee he told her about a commune in New Mexico he had lived in for four years; he was thinking about doing a chapter on it. He hadn't yet found a title for the book.

"Listen," he said when they got up, "I'm throwing a party a week from Friday, the twenty-second. Would you like to come? Stuart's going to be there."

"I'm going home on the twenty-third," she said, "early, but I'm sure I can stop in for an hour or so."

"Good," he said as they walked toward the door. "From eight o'clock on. Bring your friend if you want." He smiled at her. "I saw you smooching on the corner a while back. Give me a third-floor window and I become a real Nosy Parker."

"Who doesn't?" she said.

"Tell him for me I admire his taste. What a pity that was about Naomi—what was it, Singer?"

She stopped by the doorway, looking at him.

"The girl who jumped," he said. "Woman, I mean."

She looked at him.

"Oops," he said. "Have I spilled some beans? I only saw them together once. Eating, not smooching. In Jackson Hole."

He took his coat from the rack, said good-bye to Sara.

Turned to her. "See you on the twenty-second," he said, shaking her hand. "Very informal. Unemployed actors."

"I'm sure it'll be fun," she said, smiling.

SHE LOOKED AT the videocamera. Turned her head and stood looking at Diane's chestnut hair and its dark brown roots, at the changing number above the door. Rode up to twenty.

The phone rang as she hung her coat away. She picked Felice up and put her on her shoulder, kissed and stroked her; switched the kitchen light on, caught the phone before the third ring could start the machine. "Hello," she said.

"Hi, honey, is something wrong?"

"You tell me," she said. "About Naomi Singer, for instance." Felice purred; she petted her, kissed her furred flank.

"I'm not sure what you mean. . . ."

"Naomi Singer," she said. "You can't have forgotten her. She was around thirty, I think. Worked for Channel Thirteen." She petted Felice.

"Kay, what's this about?"

"Sam was in today," she said. "He asked me to tell you he admires your taste in women." She crouched, hitched her shoulder; Felice jumped off behind her. "He saw you with her," she said, standing. "In Jackson Hole." Switched the phone to her left ear.

"Oh. Yes, that could be, I was there with her once. . . . We went to one of those Sunday-afternoon jazz concerts at the Church of the Heavenly Rest and stopped in on the way back. You think it was some big affair I've been keeping secret? It wasn't, honey. I went out with her two times altogether, that and once before. The chemistry was wrong."

"Then why didn't you ever tell me?" she asked.

"There was nothing to tell. Did you tell me about every guy *you* had a hamburger with? She was my type physically, two on a scale of you, and she was in television, so I spoke to her in the mailroom and took her to Hanratty's for a couple of drinks. But the chemistry was wrong. She was very down and uncommunicative."

"Vida said she was bubbly." She watched Felice on her hind legs scratching at the cork doughnuts.

"Maybe she was bubbly with Vida but she was down and uncommunicative with me. Then a few weeks later she called on a Sunday and asked me to the concert, and I figured why not; it was a nice day and I might as well get out. She was still down and uncommunicative. That's the whole story. A few weeks later . . ."

She said, "You ought to have told me. I can't understand why you didn't at least mention it."

"It isn't as if I lied. You didn't ask. Look, Kay, it's not one of my favorite topics. I felt I could have listened more closely to her, noticed some signs, maybe reached out somehow."

She sighed. "You can't reproach yourself for something like that. . . ."

"I know, but that's how I felt. So I guess I don't like to stir it up. If Sam wants to talk about who did what with whom, I can tell you about some acting lessons where the scenes—" "Don't, Pete," she said, "I really don't want to know." She pounced and grabbed the water bowl as Felice bent to it; brought it to the sink and spilled the water out.

"I'm just pissed off at him for trying to make trouble between us."

She backhanded the lever. "That wasn't the case at all," she said, rinsing the bowl under the flow.

"It sounds like just what you warned me about, an old man being jealous and hostile."

"He was inviting us to a party," she said, filling the bowl. "He saw us 'smooching' on the corner. Stuart is signing him."

"Did you tell him who I am?"

"No, of course not," she said, lowering the bowl, "but he's probably going to find out. As soon as he turns in something about your mother, Stuart or Norman or someone will tell him I'm going with her son. Why don't *you* tell him? He won't necessarily catch on about the foundation." She petted Felice's head as she lapped the water. "And if he does," she said, "well, maybe it wouldn't be bad for him to know about that too."

"Come on down, we'll talk about it. Vida's back, she had the operation, and Liz is setting up for her rap group."

"Oh darn," she said. Stood, turned the water off. "I can't watch tonight," she said, "I've *got* to catch up on my reading."

"You're not still sore at me, are you?"

"No, no," she said, toeing her shoes off. "Really, baby. I'm so far behind it's pathetic. I had to bull my way through a conference today and I didn't enjoy it one bit. Come up later. Will you?"

"Sure. Love you."

"I love *you*," she said. "Do you have something to eat?"

"Plenty. See you later."

They kissed, hung up.

SHE SAT LOOKING at words on paper, wondering if he had lied to her again. He had certainly proved he was aces at it, fluent, convincing. . . .

What if the chemistry had been right or not so wrong, if he'd had an affair with Naomi Singer? Had he taken her into 13B? Had she too gotten hooked on watching? Yes, hooked was the word for it, *hooked*—on that God's-eye view of life, a sliver of it.

Was he watching *her*, now, as she sat there looking at words on paper? To see whether she was reading or wondering? Had he clicked the switches, touched the buttons, put her on 1 or 2?

She turned the page. . . .

Turning paranoid.

Except that, thanks to the video wizardry of Takai or Sakai or Banzai, he really could be watching her, could be practically reading over her shoulder. No wonder Hubert Sheer had been going to Japan to do his research. . . .

She focused on the words. So far behind it was pathetic . . .

Another serial killer. Come on, guys, give us a break.

She read a dozen pages of the manuscript. Blue-penciled the Diadem form on the agency binder, *Not for us*. Put it aside.

Felt an urge to look up at the light. Scratched her neck instead as she took the next manuscript.

Domestic conflict. Not as hairy as the Hoffmans and the McAuliffs but credible, well written, quite interesting. The phone rang.

She looked at it. Picked up on the second ring. "Hello?" she said.

"You mean it's not the machine? Ye gods, I can't believe it."

"Hi, Roxie," she said. "I'm sorry, I've been up to my ears."

"I can imagine. How *is* Young Blue-Eyes?"

"Dandy," she said. Was he listening?

"Guess who's having an exhibit at the Greene Street Gallery come April."

"Oh God, Roxie," she said, "that's terrific! Congratulations! Tell me all about it!"

Roxie did, and about Fletcher's mother's accident, and their Christmas plans, and a movie they had seen. "Are you okay?"

"Fine," she said. "Just a light-year behind in my reading."

"Why didn't you *say* something? Good-bye, good-bye. We're going ice-skating Sunday, want to come?"

"I'll speak to Pete and call you. Good-bye. Love to Fletcher." She hung up.

Sat reading.

Scratched her neck.

Took a shower.

Saw movement beyond the steamy glass. The door opened

and he came in naked, smiling. "Surprise," he said, hugging her in the downpour, wincing at its heat, dancing against her— "Owwweee . . ."

She caught her breath. "I could do without *Psycho*," she said.

"I'm sorry." He hugged her tighter, kissing her cheek. "I took a couple of peeks at you. When I saw you go in, I thought, 'Jeez, I can actually go up and get in with her.' I couldn't resist."

She said, "I knew you were watching me. . . ."

"I knew you knew," he said. Smiled. "It was sort of a turn-on. . . ." She looked away; he took her jaw and turned her face to him, looked at her. "I wasn't lying, honey," he said. "Really. I took her out twice and that was it. If it had been a big thing I would have told you. I don't blame you for wondering; look how much I've lied to you before. But it's the truth. I swear." He kissed her, hugging her.

She tongued with him in the downpour.

She hadn't known he had a passkey, though she ought to have guessed he would. Even where people had changed their locks, there would be duplicate keys in Dmitri's office that he could have access to.

FIRST THING NEXT morning she called the publicity department. Tamiko was there. "Hi dear, I need a favor," she said. "Could you get me newspaper clippings about those deaths in my building? I might as well be fully informed on the subject. The last one was near the end of October, Hubert Sheer with a double E."

"One of the databases we subscribe to ought to cover that. Did you check?"

"I didn't think of it," she said. "I never do."

"It's Thirteen Hundred Madison, right?"

"Yes."

"I'll check. If there's nothing there I'll call someone at the *Times*. No sweat either way."

"Thank you, bless you," she said.

"What's this I hear about you and a Prince Charming?"

"We're friends," she said.

When her ten-thirty appointment left the office, Sara brought in a nine-by-twelve envelope from publicity.

A computer printout, accordion-folded, half an inch thick.

She skimmed over accounts of community opposition to plans filed by Barry Beck for a 21-story sliver building at 1300 Madison Avenue; of Civitas and Carnegie Hill Neighbors up in arms, rallies at the Brick Church, a three-year battle lost in court—half of the half an inch.

She read about the death, believed to be drug-related, of William G. Webber, securities analyst, 27, of 1300 Madison Avenue.

Yes, the follow-ups reported, William G. Webber's death had been drug-related, a massive cocaine overdose. He had been a dealer as well as a user; apparently he had confused his cut and uncut merchandise. Fortunately his two female companions had taken less than he.

She hurried to an eleven o'clock marketing meeting—a love-in, what with four books on next Sunday's list, two fiction, two non. June invited her to dinner, "and Peter too, or anyone else of course," on Saturday, January sixth. She thanked her, said it would be Pete more than likely.

She lunched a British agent at Perigord East.

Told Sara to hold all calls.

Read about Naomi Singer's suicidal plunge from her fifteenth-floor apartment at 1300 Madison Avenue. The account mentioned the fatal heart attack a year earlier of another of the building's tenants, Brendan Connahay, 54, and the cocaine-overdose death before that of a third tenant, William G. Webber, 27.

Naomi Singer had been 31, a production assistant at WNET-

TV. She had called in sick on a Thursday morning and jumped from her living-room window shortly before noon. A native of Boston and a Wellesley graduate, she had moved to New York three months earlier. She left a page-long handwritten letter "expressing depression about world and personal affairs and apologizing to her family and friends." She had no history of mental illness or drug use.

The friends and co-workers of Naomi Singer, 31, who threw herself from a window at 1300 Madison Avenue, were shocked. A Barbara Ann Avakian was quoted: "Though Naomi was deeply concerned about environmental issues and human rights, she was basically a very affirmative person. She made numerous friends in the short time she was here at Thirteen, and she was enthusiastic about the project she was working on, a documentary on the homeless. It's difficult to understand how she could do such a terrible thing."

She read about the death of Rafael Ortiz, 30, the superintendent at 1300 Madison Avenue, whose head and left arm had been partially severed in an elevator motor. He had been performing routine maintenance, early on a Tuesday morning. Such accidents, while not unheard of, were rare and almost invariably associated with drug or alcohol use, according to a spokesperson for the elevator's manufacturer. Mr. Ortiz's death was the fourth in the building in slightly over two years. He left a pregnant wife and two children.

The autopsy on Rafael Ortiz, 30, partially decapitated in the elevator machinery at 1300 Madison Avenue, revealed no signs of recent drug or alcohol use.

Edgar P. Voorhees, an attorney representing the 1300 Madison Avenue Corporation, declined to comment on the rapid out-of-court settlement of the $10,000,000 lawsuit brought by the widow of the late Rafael Ortiz, 30, against the owners of the ill-starred Upper East Side sliver building. . . .

She read about the death of Hubert Sheer, 43, found in his shower at 1300 Madison Avenue.

Read again about *The Worm in the Apple*, magazine articles, teaching at Columbia, Vietnam, the U. of Chicago, the surviving parents and brothers.

Read again Martin Sugarman's comment: "He was working on what surely would have been a *magnum opus*, an overview and analysis of television's past, present, and future. His death is a loss not only for everyone who knew him but for all of society, which undoubtedly would have benefited from his insights."

The autopsy on Hubert Sheer, 43, indicated that he had drowned on the floor of his shower while unconscious as the result of a blow to the head suffered in a fall. He had taped a plastic bag around a cast on his right foot, the result of a bicycle mishap the week before. His death occurred sometime during the night of October 23–24 and was the fifth in three years at 1300 Madison Avenue, the so-called "Horror High-Rise."

She closed the printout and put her hands on it, flat, side by side. Drummed to a slow beat.

She had edited dozens of Gothics and thrillers, she reminded herself.

Fatal falls in real life were accidents more often than not, *especially* in showers.

Naomi Singer's page-long handwritten letter couldn't possibly have been a forgery.

Could it?

She sat watching her hands drumming on the flat accordion of computer printout.

She buzzed Sara and asked her to get Martin Sugarman.

Sat thumbing the edges of the accordion folds.

Too many Gothics and thrillers . . .

"Hello, Kay!"

"Hello, Martin," she said. "How are you?"

"Fine, thanks. Congratulations, you people must be walking on air over there!"

"Thanks," she said. "I haven't noticed anyone complaining. Martin, I've just reread the accounts of Hubert Sheer's death. . . ."

"Oh?"

"Do you happen to know," she asked, "whether he was planning to visit a Japanese manufacturer named Takai or Sakai? Of surveillance cameras. They're supposed to be top of the line."

"I have his list of appointments. I have all his papers relating to the book, I'm getting another writer on it. Why do you ask?"

She drew a breath. "I'm researching the five deaths in the building," she said. "There may be a book there. Could you possibly check that list for me? I'd appreciate it."

"Certainly, of course. Hold on."

She sat back, turned. Watched lights going on in the glass-walled offices across the street.

Too many Gothics and thrillers . . .

"My secretary's getting it. Kay, when I think of some of the books you've edited, it wouldn't surprise me if you thought foul play might be involved. I can tell you right now you'd be barking up the wrong tree, at least as far as Rocky's death was concerned."

"Why is that?" she asked.

"What happened is, when he slipped, he hit the side of his head against the handle of the shower, hard enough to knock him unconscious; and then, when he fell to the floor, he was sort of hunched over, on his knees, with his face down, and he breathed water into his lungs and drowned. There's no question that that's what happened; the bruise on his head matched the handle exactly. That's a very distinctive piece of hardware—you must know, you must have the same one—and there's no way in the world anyone could have pushed his head down against it hard enough to knock him out; he was a strong, healthy man despite the injured ankle. And nobody else was there, he had no visitors that night and there was no forced entry." Paper rustled. "I have the list now. What was that name again?"

She said, "Takai or Sakai. Or something like it."

"Takai or Sakai . . . Yes, the Takai Company—T, A, K, A, I—in Osaka. He was going to see them on Tuesday, October thirty-first, eight A.M. Eight—no wonder they get so much done.

He has a little note here, 'High rez cams'—high-resolution cameras, that would be. 'Cust, H, S, G, S . . .' "

She said, "Custom housings . . ."

"Yes, that would fit. Why do you ask about this one company?"

She sat silent.

"Kay?"

"It's too complicated to go into," she said. "Thank you, Martin."

"You heard what I said? It was a tragic accident, it couldn't possibly have been anything else."

She said, "I heard."

"Will you congratulate Norman and June for me?"

"Yes, I will," she said. "Thanks again, Martin. Good-bye."

She hung up.

Leaving him wondering, no doubt, about her mental health.

She wondered about it too.

Thinking that someone could take the chrome Art Deco handle from any shower in 1300 Madison Avenue, could take it off with a screwdriver probably, and—wire it or tape it or something—to a piece of two-by-four or a baseball bat or something. . . .

Pete? Petey? Her baby? Her love?

No, never, he couldn't.

He could lie, yes—small wonder, with an actress for a mother and a corporate exec for a father. But lying was a far, far cry from killing. Killing was—

Killing was a major event. . . .

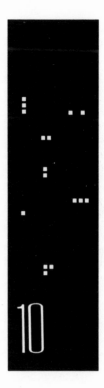

10

They watched the Wagnalls, the Bakers. The Ostrows, the week's man from the Yoshiwara Company and his guests.

She watched him watching.

He glanced at her.

She smiled. Said, "You know what I wouldn't mind taking a look at?"

"What?" he asked.

"Us," she said.

He grinned. "Thought you'd never ask." He leaned to her; they kissed. "Don't go way," he said.

He swiveled, got up, went to the foyer.

She swiveled and rolled sideward, her chair bumping his; watched him walk through the foyer and into the back room. Light went on as he went in among the cartons and what-all. He turned to the left, went from sight.

She swiveled, reaching; touched the 13A middle button, the 2 button.

Watched him on 2 moving through darkness down to the lower right of the screen. He switched the light on in his messy Conran's bedroom, closed the door. Turned to the wall and crouched down between the door and the first section of accordion-folded closet door, made a lifting movement.

His head and shoulders blocked and shadowed what he did.

He stood and turned, a dark cassette-shape in his hand.

She touched another button and the 2 button, her hand shaking. She gripped it with her left. Watched the Gruens playing bridge with two men.

She scanned the monitors. Saw Denise arguing with Kim in the 5B living room, put them on 1. "—*job*, I'm not going to jeopardize it for a measly five hundred dollars!" Denise said, throwing her napkin on the table, getting up and going to the window. "Do you think I'm an idiot?" "Now comes the good stuff," he said, coming in. She put a hand up.

"Will you for once use your head, Denise?" Kim said, pouring cream into her coffee.

He sat, swiveled, taking a cassette from its black slipcase.

"You could wind up making four or five thousand," Kim said. "Even more. And no taxes. May I please smoke one effing cigarette?"

They watched Denise and Kim.

The Bakers, the Coles.

She watched him press a button on the right-hand VCR, feed the cassette into the opening and home it, press other buttons, click a switch in the center bank.

They watched themselves on 2.

"Jesus, I'm *fat*," she said.

"You are not," he said, "you're gorgeous. . . ."

"Oh God, baby, that feels good," she said, lying back across the bed, his hand caressing her right breast, his head over the other.

He took her arm; she got up, watching; moved over, sat in his lap.

They watched Kay and Pete.

SHE DECIDED TO make the next day, Friday, an at-home day. She hadn't planned to but she was too tired to get up early.

"I have to go out this afternoon," he said, leaning over an elbow on the counter, watching a muffin in the microwave, Felice standing on his back sniffing at the cabinets.

"Just as well," she said, pouring the coffee. "I've really *really* got to do some work. Where are you going?"

"Ohh . . . downtown," he said, smiling. "Christmassy stuff. Nothing involving anybody you know."

He helped her clean up. They kissed at the door. "Call before you go," she said.

He smiled at her. "Love you," he said.

"I love *you*, Pete," she said, looking into his eyes.

They kissed.

She called Sara and asked her to make cancellations and apologies, new appointments.

"Are you all right?"

"Fine," she said. "Just farther behind than I realized."

Not to mention turning paranoid.

With no Christmas shopping done yet either.

She read at the desk. Felice slept on the bed.

He called at 1:37. "How you doing?"

"Okay," she said. "I've really made some headway."

"Bad news. Allan got the ax."

"Damn," she said. "Those bastards . . ."

"The whole department practically."

"How's he taking it?" she asked.

"He's fine; Babette is having hysterics. I'm leaving now. I should be back around five."

She said, "I was just thinking about maybe coming down and watching while I eat a yogurt. . . ."

"Do you want to? I'll leave the key for you, behind the mirror."

"Would you?" she said. "I think I will."

"You know how to start up, don't you?"

"Yes," she said.

"See you later." A kiss.

She kissed. "Love you," she said.

"Me too." Kiss, kiss.

She hung up.

Sat looking at the page before her.

Tried again to think of a present for him. Maybe something for those bare walls.

She read a few minutes, then turned the lamp off, the machine on. Got up, went to the bathroom, washed. Got her keys.

Told Felice she'd be back in a while.

Took the stairs down to thirteen.

She didn't look too bad, all things considered. She drew a bottom corner of the mirror's gilt frame farther from the black-and-white-checked wall. The key missed her cupped fingers, bounced on the table, a tiny crescent gouged in the tan lacquer by the cylindrical tip. She fingertipped her tongue, rubbed the lacquer. The nick stayed.

She unlocked 13B, went in.

Switched on the foyer light as she closed the door; pocketed the key. Looked at the gray screens gleaming in the living room, at the kitchen, the half-open doors to the dark bathroom and dim back room.

She went to the back-room door and opened it. The blind's narrow slats were edged with sunshine, lighting the workbench and its tools and dismantled monitors, the transformer's metal doghouse in the corner by the window, the rowing machine, cartons, odds and ends of scrap lumber. . . .

She went to the center closet, drew the accordion doors apart. Reached in and pulled the plywood door open. Ducked and went through—parting clothes and accordion doors—into the sunny blue-and-tan Conran's bedroom. The blind was up most of the way, the window open an inch or so at either side.

She surveyed the clothes-strewn room. "*Pete?*" she called.

She went to the door.

Looked out across the foyer into the living room—the side of the tan leather sofa, blue sky above a building over on Park.

She closed the door. Turned to the wall and crouched.

Felt the parquet floor before her. The wood pieces were smooth, tight-fitting. She pushed, pressed; nothing slid or yielded.

She tried the baseboard—three or four inches high, some thirty inches long—grasped at it and pulled. It held firm, though a hairline crack divided it from the white wall. She pressed an end of the board, pressed the other end.

Remembered his movement. Lifted.

The board came up and off, grooves at either end sliding on metal tongues in the door and closet-door frames.

She put the board down beside her and raised a gray metal handle in the opening, drew out a wide shallow gray-metal drawer. Hundred- and five-hundred-dollar bills lay in it, five paper-banded sheaves—three of one hundreds, two of fives. A maroon leather box the size of a cigar box, manila envelopes. Cassettes.

Three black slipcases lying side by side on others.

She picked one up; a K was penned on the label on the spine.

The next cassette, labeled K2, was the one they had watched the night before; she picked it up. The next cassette was labeled R. Rocky?

Four cassettes were in the lower layer: N, N2, N3, and B.

Which puzzled her till she remembered that William G. Webber, 27, was Billy Webber.

She crouched there, looking at the cassettes in her hands. Afraid she hadn't been paranoid at all.

HE SHOULD HAVE allowed longer than twenty minutes, a Friday a little over a week before Christmas; they were rolling past Seventy-second Street and the watch said 1:55 already.

But hey, it was a Checker cab, a relic from the past, with plenty of space and a pulled-down jump seat to put the feet on. Easy listening on the radio. So he'd be late; they would wait for him. . . .

He was on his way to the Pace Gallery to choose between two Hoppers. Then Tiffany's.

He smiled, his feet up, his hands folded.

Lovely to think of her back there watching on her own. His love enjoying his other love . . .

Who would ever have thought he'd have a woman he could share it with, could actually entrust it to for a while? A woman so perfect, so loving. How right he had been to risk showing it to her. He breathed a sigh. Was anyone luckier?

And just the other night, thanks to Sam that bastard, he'd been shivering on the precipice. What a moment that had been, when she asked him out of nowhere to tell her about Naomi. Yeow!

Thank God he'd been able to convince her he wasn't hiding anything. Last night clinched it, the way she'd been so open and into everything, wanting to watch *them*, so with it when they did. . . .

Two firsts for her: watching them, and watching alone now . . .

He took his feet off the jump seat.

Sat up, cold inside.

Turned and looked out. A Doberman eyed him from the open window of a limo alongside, paws resting on gleaming black.

He turned the other way. Watched the Frick Museum sliding by . . .

Could she have watched *him* when he was getting the cassette?

Of course she could have, dummy.

Was *that* why she had asked to see the tape? Had she somehow guessed the truth about Naomi, *all* of it? Guessed too—so goddamn smart she was—that he had taped it, and stashed the tape of them in the same place?

She was watching alone on a Friday at-home day, another first—and it was on the clipboard: the address, the day, the time. He hadn't written *Pace Gallery* precisely because she would be able to see it and maybe guess what he was getting her.

Shit. Top of the world two seconds ago and whammo, paranoid again.

He faced front, leaned forward. Squinted through the smoggy plastic barrier and the windshield beyond at the four-lane lava flow of cabs and buses oozing down Fifth Avenue. "Jesus," he said, "what a goddamn fucking *mess*."

"It's a gridlock alert day," the driver said.

He drew breath and hissed it out, shaking his head. "This goddamn city," he said.

Sat back.

Stuck his feet up on the jump seat.

Studied the Reeboks this way and that.

Played with the muffler's woolly fringe, listened to the easy listening.

Icy inside.

The way she'd watched his hands when he put the cassette in and switched over . . .

Was she putting a cassette in right that moment? N3?

Horns honked. Traffic was frozen.

"You want to cut over to Park?" the driver asked.

■　　■　　■

SHE FAST-FORWARDED; the bathroom stayed empty behind white streaks, the cane leaning by the shower door. At the top of the screen someone there and gone.

She stopped, rewound.

Played.

The bathroom was empty, the cane leaning by the shower door, the sound of the shower vibrant. Legs in jeans and sneakers passed outside the foyer doorway, from right to left.

Returned, crouched.

She froze Pete.

Crouching in the doorway in a striped rugby shirt, a hand low before him as if to pitch a coin.

She watched him—and let him move. He pitched, stood. Stepped aside and was gone.

She watched the empty bathroom. Couldn't make out the tiny something he had pitched onto the black floor a few feet in from the door, by the bath mat. Whatever it was, he was there in Hubert "Rocky" Sheer's apartment. About to kill him.

Pete. Her baby, her love.

She closed her eyes.

Opened them. Watched the shower door open, Sheer's hand take the towel from the hook.

She fast-forwarded—till he hobbled out with the towel around him, lifting his glare-wrapped foot over the sill, taking the cane, shifting it to his right hand. He stepped forward and stopped on the mat, head down. Bent over the cane and his left leg, the glary foot rising behind him, his left hand reaching down. His head turned toward the doorway as Pete, with both hands, slashed down a glinting club. She killed the sound, shut her eyes, rolled away swiveling.

Sat holding her fist, biting her thumb knuckle.

He had killed the others too, he must have; had been afraid that Sheer, who made connections . . . would make connections.

She opened her eyes to the blue-white brightness of the left-hand monitors. Chris and Sally, Pam, Jay, Lauren. A man she hadn't seen before on Dr. Palme's couch.

She drew a breath.

Looked over at 2. He was leaning over Sheer's head and shoulders, astride his back as he lay sprawled on the floor. A halo shone in flashes around Sheer's head—a metal-foil pan beneath it.

He was drowning him. . . .

She rolled, reached, stopped the tape, sprang the VCR's opening.

Took the cassette out and put it down by its case.

Looked at the half dozen other cassettes on the console.

The blue digits said 2:06. Plenty of time to look at some of N3 and B; he'd barely have gotten to wherever he was going on Fifty-seventh Street.

But no, he might come back early and surprise her in the act, as in too many Gothics and thrillers—his appointment cut short for some reason, another part of the infrastructure crumbled. Let the police look at N3 and B later; now was the time to get out, taking the tapes with her, out of there and out of the building. Leaving an ordinary everyday note so he wouldn't panic and run, or do something worse.

He was mad. Had to be. A sociopath despite his charm, his humor, the love he'd given her—and he did love her, she was sure of that. The killings must have all sprung from the need to keep the cameras secret. Protecting his six-million-dollar toy—*his* baby—that she had been so quick to share.

She bowed her head, rubbing it.

Sat up, combed her hair back with both hands, drew a breath.

Looked at the cassettes.

Rolling to the right, she bumped his chair away; opened a bottom drawer, gathered slipcased cassettes, seven, from the rows inside.

She exchanged the cassettes in the two sets of cases, trying to think about what to put in the note and where the police station was, not about his arrest and the media onslaught that would follow, the headlines, the microphones, the public exposure. She double-checked the labels on the K and K2 cassettes; those weren't going to the police, those she would hide upstairs and break open later and destroy. She took the pen, marked their new cases.

She brought the stack of wrong-cassettes-in-right-cases through the foyer and into the back room; through the closets, into his bedroom.

Crouching, she stocked the shallow gray drawer the way she had found it, the N's and B on the bottom, the K's and R above—alongside the maroon leather box, the envelopes, the sheaves of one-hundred- and five-hundred-dollar bills.

She peeked into the box—gold coins, mounted sets. She closed it, pushed the drawer into its recess. Replaced the baseboard, slid it down tight to the floor.

She stood and opened the door, swung it to the wall, wondering how much his money, his never-mentioned money, had softened her judgment, blinded her to things she might otherwise have picked up on.

She backed through the closets, drawing closed the accordion doors to the bedroom, swinging closed the plywood door, drawing closed the accordion doors in the back room.

She went through the foyer into the living room, to the console. Stacked up the right-cassettes-in-wrong-cases. Drew the clipboard to her, turned back the top yellow sheet, took the pen. Stood leaning over the console, frowning at the pad. A meeting, suddenly called, at which her presence was urgently required? Fishy . . .

She looked up, squinted for something better—at him in the number-two elevator in his coat and striped muffler, a woman with him. She stared. Put it on 2; it stayed blank, she found the switch.

He stood in the elevator, looking pained, rubbing behind his neck, the overcoat open. The Stangersons' maid moved forward, ready to step off. On ten.

She dropped the pen, opened the bottom drawer on the right, grabbed the stacked cassettes and put them down in with the others. Closed the drawer, fixed the chairs, the clipboard, put

Dr. Palme on 1, switched the sound on, made for the foyer; turned back, leaned, slapped shut the VCR and turned it off, hurried to the foyer; opened the door as he came out of the elevator. "What's wrong?" she asked.

He winced at her, rubbing behind his neck. "My cab was in an accident," he said, his voice shaky.

"Oh Lord," she said. "Are you all right?" Stepped forward.

"I don't know." He moved to her as the elevator door slid closed. "I think so. I got thrown around and I was seeing double for a while but it's clearing up now." He blinked a few times.

"Did you hurt your neck?" she asked.

"Yeah, a little," he said.

She turned him around. He pulled the muffler off as she patted at the back of his neck.

"Your hands are shaking."

She said, "I could see in the elevator something was wrong. Just the fact you were back so soon. What happened?"

"A guy pulled out of a parking space without looking; we ran into him. On Fifth, near Seventy-ninth Street. A New Jersey driver, of course. It was a Checker cab, so I really got thrown around." He shook a leg, drew breath hissingly.

"Gee *whiz* . . ." she said, pressing at his neck, rubbing it.

"The car was a brand-new Mercedes."

"Was anyone badly hurt?" she asked.

"The passenger in the car. A woman. Her leg was crushed."

"You ought to go to a doctor and get checked over," she said.

He turned around. "If anything hurts tomorrow, I will," he said.

"Do you have someone here?" she asked.

He nodded.

They looked at each other. She touched the edge of his open coat. "Poor Pete," she said. Smiled at him. Took him in her arms.

He hugged her. "I should have just gone in someplace and sat awhile," he said. "It was dumb to come back."

"No," she said, "you were right to."

They smiled at each other.
Kissed.

THEY WENT INTO 13B. He closed the door. "Have you had your yogurt yet?" he asked, getting out of the coat. Winced.

"Ooh," she said. Helped him from behind. "No, I just got down here," she said. "Norman called after you did. I have to go in in a little while."

"You do?" he said, turning, taking the coat.

"I was going to leave you a note," she said. "He's got Anne Tyler coming in at four and he wants me to be there. She isn't happy where she is now."

"It would be nice having *her* on the list," he said, rubbing his sweatered shoulder.

"Wouldn't it though," she said. "He feels there's a good chance. He and June have known her for years." She went into the kitchen.

"Let me have one too, hon."

She looked into the refrigerator. "Lemon or blueberry?" she asked.

"Blueberry. New patient with Dr. Palme."

"I know." She took out two yogurts, elbowed the door, got spoons, napkins.

He was in his chair, the phone at his cheek, when she came in.

He smiled at her as she put a cup, spoon, and napkin before him. "This is Peter Henderson," he said. "I had an appointment for two o'clock. . . . Right."

She sat, putting her spoon and napkin down, watching the masters.

"I was in an accident just now," he said, tucking the phone in his shoulder. "On the way down there. I got a little shaken up. Could we make it Monday, the same time?"

They opened their cups, watching the masters. Dr. Palme said, "If it's so inconsequential, why are you here?"

"It's Linda's idea," the man on the couch said.

"Even better," Pete said. "I'm sorry about today. Good-bye." He hung up. Made a note on the clipboard. "A place that sells paintings on velvet," he said.

She whistled.

They ate their yogurt, watching Dr. Palme, Lauren, Jay, the Hoffmans.

"I've got to get moving," she said, standing up. She gathered the cups with the spoons and napkins in them, the lids. "Are you sure you're all right?"

"Fine," he said, taking his hand from the back of his neck, watching.

"Your eyes are okay?"

He nodded.

"I'll be back by six," she said, "unless we go for drinks." She bent, kissed his head. He turned his face up to her. They kissed lips.

She went into the kitchen, put the cups and napkins in the garbage, rinsed the spoons, put them in the rack. Went into the foyer, opened the door. "Oh, the key," she said.

"Keep it, honey," he said, swiveling. "It's a spare one."

Her hand in her pocket, she looked at him sitting dark before the blue-white screens, the hanging sea-green lamp. "*Merci*," she said. "Fair enough, since you've got one to my place."

"That's what I was thinking," he said. Kissed at her. "I hope it goes well."

"Thanks." She kissed at him. "You ought to take a hot bath," she said. "A long one, otherwise you're really going to be sore later on."

"You're right," he said. "I will, I just want to see Jay's reaction."

They smiled at each other. She opened the door and went out.

Closed the door.

Moved to the elevators, touched the up button. Drew a breath.

Was he lying again? Had he come back because he'd been afraid of her being there alone? But then he wouldn't have left the key, or given it to her now. Easy enough for the champion liar to invent excuses . . .

He had *seemed* shaken up. And coming back home to Mommy fit psychologically. Thank God she hadn't watched the tapes longer, had closed the baseboard drawer. The cassettes, the right ones, would be safe enough where they were; he was hardly likely to play one.

He probably *had* been on his way to an art gallery; Fifty-seventh Street was loaded with them. Buying her a Hopper or a Magritte, no doubt. She sighed, shook her head.

Gave the camera in the elevator a smile.

The thing to do was stay calm and act the way she would if she were going to meet with Norman and Anne Tyler, if only. Nothing to make him uneasy if he was watching. Calling 911 was out; he could be up there before they answered. A confrontation was the last thing she wanted.

Felice rubbed against her ankle as she turned the door bolt. "Hi, sweets," she said, picking her up; kissed her nose and put her on her shoulder, stroked her as she went into the bedroom. The machine's red light sparked—visible on the masters. If he was watching.

She spilled Felice onto the bed and went to the desk. One message, the machine's indicator said. She touched the playback button, praying it wouldn't be Sara saying the wrong thing.

A woman from Bloomingdale's told her that the coffee table would be delayed two more weeks; they were sorry.

She turned the radio on, went to the window. Eyed the gray sky above the brown park. Felice, on the windowsill, nuzzled her knee; she scratched Felice's head. A newscaster told about a shooting in the subway. She went to the closets, unbuttoning her shirt. Opened accordion doors.

She chose the blue wool dress—okay for Anne Tyler, fine for

the police. Laid it out on the bed, pushing Felice away. Got panty hose from the dresser, a half-slip, a bra.

Shower?

Would he notice if she didn't? Think it odd? Wonder why she was suddenly skipping the goddamn shower?

If he was watching . . .

Would he wonder enough to go check his cassettes? The cassettes, not the cases? Unlikely. But if he did, he could stop the elevator at thirteen when she was leaving. . . .

She undressed. The newscaster talked about snow on its way from western Pennsylvania, four to eight inches. She turned the radio off.

Went into the bathroom. Put the shower cap on. Felice scratched in the litter box.

She leaned in at the shower door, grasped the chrome Art Deco handle, turned it. Its twin from 13A or B had surely been the glint on that slashing club or bat or whatever. The police would probably still be able to find marks on it, microscopic scratches.

She felt the water, turned it hotter.

Stepped into the black glass stall, drew the door closed.

Made it a quickie. Marveled as she scrubbed that the Pete she had loved—still loved, hated, pitied—could be the same Pete who had swung that brutal blow, had drowned Sheer there on the floor. . . .

He must have spent hours fixing things right and cleaning up—all of it on tape. A major event—on the night before that glorious morning when she had circled the reservoir and bumped into Sam, and would *he* be astounded when he heard the whole story. A change in the light outside the steamy door?

She wiped a hand across it, peered out—at the empty bathroom.

Her imagination.

She rinsed off. Calmly. Going to meet with Norman and Anne Tyler. June too, of course.

She opened the door, took the towel from the hook.

Dried herself, took off the shower cap, hung it on the handle; went out. Nothing on the floor by the bath mat.

She finished drying at the sink, looking in the mirror at herself, not at the light up behind her.

She went into the bedroom, sat on the bed and put on the panty hose; stood, worked them up, snugged them. Put on the bra, caught her breasts in it; went to the window, hooking the strap behind her.

She stood looking at the gray sky, adjusting the bra. Snow on the way, all right. The reservoir was wind-ruffled, a few joggers on the track beyond it.

She moved to the end of the window, drew the draperies. The green-and-white chintz panels swept together, brushing against the edge of the windowsill, bare except for the telescope.

She went into the bathroom, put on minimal makeup. Should have said she was going to help Roxie move furniture . . .

She thought about the chaos ahead, the trial, the media piranhas in a feeding frenzy, biting not only at Pete but at her too, the older woman taken in by the so-much-younger man. Sweet Jesus, the hypocritical sympathy she'd be getting from men *and* women, the smirks behind her back. She longed to talk with Roxie ("Got a problem, Rox, Pete's a murderer"). Sirens far away screamed louder, coming up Madison.

Screamed louder, klaxons barking, screamed right outside; whooped and moaned low, engines throbbing.

She went into the living room, brushing at her hair. Went to the window, stood close against the sill, a hand to the upright bronze framing at its middle; leaned her forehead to the glass.

Red lights spun far below, fire engines in front of the Wales, tiny figures scurrying into its base.

She scanned the red-swept front of the hotel, its roof—no smoke or flames.

A false alarm, she hoped. Fine, it would distract him.

She moved to the end of the window, drew the draperies. The

white silk panels swept together, brushing against the edge of the windowsill.

She went back through the living room, detoured into the kitchen to shut the faucet tight, went into the bathroom.

Realized, finishing her hair, that books were going to be written about the case—and Diadem without a true-crime writer, more the pity. Although . . . whether she wanted it or not, as a major participant she was going to be in a fantastic bargaining position. If one of the big names was amenable to moving . . .

Talk about looking on the bright side . . .

She went into the bedroom, picked up the slip. The phone rang. She caught the night table's handset. "Hello?" she said, ready to cut Sara short.

"Hi."

She said, "Hi. Excitement across the street."

"It was a false alarm."

"What's up?" she asked.

"Kay . . . I can't let you go out, or call anyone."

She stood holding the phone. Said, "What are you talking about?"

"Oh honey, please . . . You know. The cassettes. Listen."

She listened.

Heard purring.

STARED AT THE draperies, the door.

Hadn't seen Felice since—before the shower—

She drew breath. Turned, sat on the side of the bed. "Pete, don't hurt her," she said.

"She's lying here in my lap and I'm tickling her ears with an X-acto knife. You know what that is, don't you? Like a pen, but with a pointy razor at the tip; I used it on the labels. The orange ear, twitch . . . The white ear, twitch . . ."

"Pete, please . . ." she said.

"I don't want to use it on her but if you don't do exactly what I tell you, I will. I need some time. To think things out."

"Fine," she said. "You can have all the time you want." She turned around, looked up toward the light beyond the foot of the bed. "Just don't hurt her," she said. "I know you won't, you love her." She looked at the light's chrome iris, at her upside-down self sitting stuck to the upside-down bed, holding the white speck of phone.

"I'll do it if you make me, Kay, I promise you."

"You can have all the time you want," she said to the light.

"You were going to the police. If I'd gotten back five minutes later those would have been *their* sirens before."

"No, I don't know what I was going to do," she said. "I wanted to get out somewhere and do some thinking myself, without being watched."

"Don't shit me, Kay. You were going to take the tapes to the police, that's why you switched them."

"I was going to hide them up here," she said. "I didn't know *what* to do. I wanted to talk with you, to hear—why you did what you did, to try to understand, but I was afraid. I thought having the tapes would give me some security. That's why I was taking them."

"You're going to do what I tell you, otherwise Felice gets it. I know which tape you watched and how much, you didn't rewind, so you know I'll really do it if I have to, don't you?"

"Yes," she said to the light. "I do."

"I need time to think. You can put some clothes on and you can work if you want—on the bed, I can see you better. If the phone rings, don't touch it, let the machine take it. And you only pick up if it's me. Got it?"

"Yes," she said.

"Is the machine set right, so you can hear who's calling?"

"Yes," she said.

"We'll talk later. I want to. Put your jeans on, or whatever you want."

"Were you really in an accident?" she asked.

"No. It dawned on me what you were up to. Do you know where I was going? To buy you a Hopper. Now look at us."

"Don't blame me," she said to the light.

"Why not, you invaded my privacy, didn't you? It's ironic, isn't it? I guess it makes us even, more or less. Go on, get dressed. And remember, don't touch the phone unless it's me. And don't get up without asking. Don't do anything that'll— rock the boat. I'll be watching you every second."

EVEN, MORE OR LESS...

Except for a few murders on his part, and menacing Felice with a razor knife—if he wasn't lying again.

Probably wasn't, having done what he'd done to Sheer.

She shivered. Hoped it looked like a reaction to the book she was holding open before her. Calm . . .

As long as he was willing to talk, as long as he was thinking things out, everything could end peacefully with nobody hurt— not Felice, not her, not him either. He couldn't hope to kill her and pass it off as an accident or suicide, not so soon after Sheer's death. And once murder was suspected, he, her lover, was bound to be the leading suspect. His owning the building would be discovered, and the screens in 13B, the cameras; all the deaths would be reinvestigated. Surely he would see it, or could be made to see it. His best bet, his only bet, was to turn himself in, hire one of the superstar lawyers, plead insanity. . . .

But what if, being insane, he *didn't* see it?

If she ran, he could cut her off, on the stairs or in the elevators. If she called the police or threw a chair through the window, he'd be the first one up there, with his passkey. . . .

Felice purring in his lap . . .

Damn him. There *had* to be a way to outwit him if he wouldn't see reason. . . .

Think Gothic. . . .

HE WATCHED HER pretending to read.

She was thinking, bet your bippy, about how to get him to go to the Nineteenth Precinct with her and turn himself in. Plead insanity.

Why the hell had she had to go snooping where she didn't belong? They'd had it all, or could have, and zap—nothing.

No question about what he had to do now, whether he wanted to or not.

She'd really left him no choice.

But how?

Not a chance in a million of getting away with another fake accident or suicide, not so soon after Rocky. And the minute the cops started thinking murder, he would be the number-one suspect, the boyfriend or husband always was (and rightly so, eh Dad?). Everything would unravel, everything. . . .

Unless . . .

The cops thought somebody else had murdered her . . . Were *sure* somebody else had. . . .

He looked to the left.

Touched the 3B top button, the 1 button.

Felice squirmed in his lap; he raised his hand. She jumped to the floor, prowled away sniffing.

He put the X-acto knife on the console. Took some jelly beans.

Leaned back, chewing, watching the masters.

Sam on 1, her on 2 . . .

It took him a minute or so to work it out. The shape, not the details.

Two big questions: could he leave her unwatched for fifteen or twenty minutes tonight while Sam was out seeing Candace's

play? And could he keep her quiet and under control till tomorrow night, the soonest he could hope to set it up for?

Salvation if he could swing it. Neat too—in both senses, neat-
cool and neat-neat. Two birds with one stone . . .

He watched them.

Sam on 1, jabbing away at the old portable. Kay on 2, turning
pages . . .

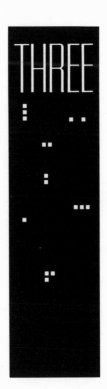

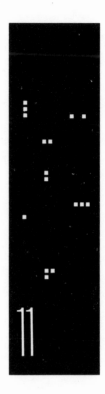

11

She closed the book. Took her glasses off, looked up at the light. Said, "I'd like to go in the kitchen and get a cup of coffee."

She sat looking at the light.

At the book, front and back.

The phone rang.

She turned to the night table—4:22 on the clock. The phone rang.

She put the glasses on the table, the book on the stack beneath, sat up. The phone rang; the machine atop the desk clicked. She combed her hands through her hair. "Hello," her voice said. "I

can't come to the phone right now, but if you'll leave your
message when the beep sounds, I'll return your call as soon as
possible. Thank you."

The machine beeped.

"It's me," his voice said.

She picked up the phone. "May I?" she said.

"Let's wait till the machine cuts off."

She sighed. Sat looking at the draperies, the desk, the light.
At Tiny holding the phone . . .

Beep.

"Yes, you can get coffee. Don't hang up, leave the phone on
the bed. I won't be able to see you in there but I've got an eye
on the lobby. If you pick up the house phone, I'll see Terry go
over and answer it; the instant he says 'Yes, Miss Norris,' Felice
gets a cut, and if he—" "Forget it," she said, "I'll get water from
the bathroom. I assume that's permitted."

"If you want coffee, you can have coffee, just don't touch the
house phone, that's all."

"I wasn't planning to," she said.

"Go ahead."

She put the phone down, got up from the bed.

Went to the kitchen, switched the light on. Looked, as the
fluorescents pinged to brightness, at the food and water bowls
on the floor in the corner, the scratching post on the wall.

The wall phone, the house phone . . .

She ran water into the teakettle, set it on a burner, turned the
flame wide beneath it. Spooned instant coffee into the mug with
the big brown K on it.

Stood watching the humming kettle. Glanced at the knife
rack.

She brought the mug into the bedroom. Picked the phone up,
sat on the side of the bed, put the phone to her ear.

"I made some too."

"Isn't that nice," she said. "We'll have a kaffeeklatsch." She
sipped.

"Honey, I'm sorry, I need some time. I don't know what the hell to do. . . ."

She shifted around, putting a folded leg onto the bed; looked up at the light. Shook her head. Sighed. "Oh God, Pete . . ." she said. "Was it because you were afraid he was going to find out about the cameras? Sheer?"

She sat looking at the light. "Was that why, Petey?" she asked.

A sigh. "Yes . . . He was going to go to the Takai showroom. He'd have seen one of the lights there, or a picture, blown the whistle. . . ."

She said, "And then the other deaths would have been reex-amined. . . ."

She sat looking at the light, holding the mug, the phone.

"I don't think I should be talking any more about this. You're liable to wind up repeating it in court."

She drank. Looked at the light. "Petey," she said, "you know you can't go on—doing what you've done. You'll get caught sooner or later, and the later it is, the worse it's going to be."

"You want me to turn myself in. . . ."

"Yes, I think it would make sense," she said. "It would count in your favor—strongly, I'm sure—and you can afford to get one of the top trial lawyers. They'll be fighting to represent you, they're all such publicity hounds."

"Oh yeah, there would be publicity, all right. Can you imagine how it would be?"

She sighed, shrugged a shoulder. "I still think it's the best thing for you to do," she said. "The only thing." She sipped, looking at the light.

"I could jump."

"Oh don't say that, baby, *no*," she said, leaning forward, shaking her head. "If everything you did was done because of the cameras—and it was, ultimately, wasn't it?" She looked at the light. "Wasn't it?"

"Yes . . ."

She said, "Baby, I'm *sure*, in light of who your mother was and all, a good lawyer could . . . make a convincing case for . . . a plea of insanity. . . ."

"You mean I could get to spend my life in a hospital? Be Hinckley's roommate?"

"Not your *life*," she said. "Maybe just a few years if you turn yourself in. You're young, you'll still have a future. And you'll be alive. Don't talk about jumping, that would be *really stupid*."

"Oh . . . shit. I've got to think. It's a tough decision. . . ."

"Of course it is," she said. "Take your time. I wasn't planning on going out tonight." She smiled. "Why don't you bring Felice back up now? She's probably getting hungry." She sat smiling at the light.

"No. I'm keeping her here. So you don't make the decision for me. I want to make my own decisions."

"All right," she said. "I can understand that."

"There's stuff here she can eat. She's having a ball, sniffing all over the place. I put some paper in the shower for her."

"She could get in trouble in the back room."

"I closed the door. She's fine—as long as you don't push me, Kay. I mean it."

"Okay," she said to the light. Nodded.

"You don't have to stay on the bed. Just keep away from the phones and the windows and the door. I'll call later. Wait till you know it's me." A click. The dial tone.

She turned, hung up.

Sat looking at the mug.

THE SNOW HAD started. People were coming into the lobby brushing it from their shoulders.

He watched Sam getting into his duffel coat. Kay, sitting against the right end of the sofa, hugging her jeaned knees, bare feet up on the cushion. She nibbled at a sidepiece of her glasses, the manuscript she'd been reading tucked down at her side.

He broke a fortune cookie open, pulled out the paper strip, held it toward the blue-white light. *The greater part of inspiration is perspiration.*

Right again, Jolly Chan. He crushed it, tossed it on the plate.

Ate a piece of the cookie, watching Sam come out of the stairway door and walk the path of dark floor mat across the lobby, saying something to Walt by the front door.

Kay reached, put the glasses on the coffee table. Looked up at him, hugging her knees. Breathed a sigh. "Call me, will you?" she said. "I think you know the number."

He watched her looking at him. Picked the phone up, touched the auto-dial button and 1.

Heard the beeps, got a busy signal. Her phone rang. She reached, stayed her hand, looking at him.

He drew a breath. Hung up, switched her phone link on.

She sat back as the phone rang. Played with a shirt button. Good angle for the cleavage . . . "Hello. I can't come to the phone right now, but if you'll leave your message . . ." Good light too.

Beep.

"Hi, it's Roxie. You there?"

She sat up, holding the sofa's back, leaning her head toward the foyer.

"The skating is off, Fletcher has to go to Atlanta. Unless you guys want to anyway. If you wanted to originally. Let me know. 'Bye." A kiss. The machine's click.

She looked up at him. "Pete?" she said.

He picked up the phone, touched the redial button.

She lowered her head, sat still.

The phone rang.

She sat back against the sofa arm. Stretched her legs out, crossed them at the ankles. Played with the shirt button while the phone rang, the message played. The jeans molded her hips and thighs, the V between . . .

Beep.

"*It's me,*" he called.

She reached, picked up the phone, leaned back.

They waited. She played with the shirt button, lying there on the Cupid's-bow sofa with her legs crossed at the ankles, holding the phone. . . .

Beep.

"Hi," she said, looking at him.

"Hi," he said, watching her.

She sighed. "I've been thinking about what it's going to be like," she said. "The publicity. The piranhas. For months, through a long trial, and after . . . The smirks I'll be getting behind my back from everyone in the office, everyone I know. The years out of your life, more than likely . . ." She sighed. "The more I think about it, the worse it all seems." She looked at him.

He watched her.

"Baby," she said, "I have an idea that may be a much happier way out of this."

"What's that?" he asked.

"Brace yourself," she said. "It's going to surprise you, but I think we ought to give it some serious thought."

"I'm braced," he said.

"What if we got married?" she said.

He looked at her looking at him. "You're right," he said, "it's a surprise."

"What it would do for *me*," she said, "among other things, is relieve me of the feeling that I have to *tell*. As long as spouses don't have to testify against each other, then they shouldn't be expected to blow the whistle on each other either, should they? It's not as if you're some crazy serial killer who did it for kicks or because of a compulsion, and might do it again. You were threatened, you were defending yourself, you had rational motives. At least that's what I'm assuming was—always the case. Correct me if I'm wrong."

Watching her, he said, "Go on . . ."

"Naturally," she said, "there would have to be some very definite preconditions, number one being an absolute shutting down of the system, at once, with no waffling about it—on my part either. We've got to recognize that someone will *always* be finding out or becoming a threat in one way or another."

He watched her. "Number two?" he said.

"I don't know," she said. "I haven't thought it all out yet. But Jesus, Pete, is either one of us ever likely to find anyone else so right? The fun we have together, the fantastic sex . . . You're still *you*, regardless; I can't switch off my feelings just like that. And I've been doing some soul-searching. Don't think I'm totally blind to the money, because I'm not, believe me. Condition Two will probably be that we get a big apartment on Park and a staff of three." She smiled. "What do you think?"

He said, "It sounds great. . . . But how do I know you mean it? You could be conning me. Maybe the minute we step outside you'll start screaming for the police."

She sighed, playing with the shirt button. "I suppose you've got to consider the possibility," she said. "Frankly my first reaction *was* to—try to think of a ploy of some kind. But Pete, the more I think about the media, and the trial—my God, it would be the biggest in years—and the piece out of your life . . . What for? What's done is done, it's not going to be *un*done. If I didn't feel obliged to tell . . ." She sighed, shook her head. "No, I'm not conning you, baby," she said. "All women aren't actresses. Will you please give it some serious thought? On the down side it means you'd probably have to settle for cats instead of children. . . ."

"That's a plus," he said.

She uncrossed her ankles, lifted a knee, looked at him, the phone to her cheek. "What were you going to get?" she asked. "A sketch?"

"A painting," he said, watching her. "They have two for me to look at."

She sighed, shook her head. "I was going to get *you* a painting," she said, playing with the shirt button. "Or some super photograph . . ."

He watched her. "Do you have enough to eat?" he asked.

"Mm-hmm," she said. "I'm dieting."

"Felice had shrimp with lobster sauce."

"Great, you're going to spoil her. . . ."

"She's sleeping under the console," he said. "With the pig."

She smiled. Rubbed at the side of her neck. Winced.
"Ooch . . ." she said. "All this has got me so goddamn *tight*. . . ."

He said, "Why don't you take a bath?"

She looked at him, smiled. "Good idea," she said.

"We'll talk afterwards," he said.

"Okay," she said.

He watched her looking at him.

They hung up.

HE GOT READY while she did.

Reread the note, changed *lover* to *stud*, folded it. Stood,
tucking it into his right hip pocket. She was running the water,
squeezing in the bubble bath.

He opened the bottom drawer on the left, found the box of
plastic gloves; tore two from the roll, put them into his left side
pocket. Checked his keys, the change in his right side pocket.

She put a cassette in the bedroom player. Segovia's guitar
struck a chord.

He watched her undress.

Not looking at him. Not a glance.

As if nobody could possibly be watching her, there in her
cozy bedroom.

Like in the old days. Only now she knew. . . .

A definite turn-on . . .

For her too?

Was she maybe, just maybe, *not* trying to con him, she with
those beautiful tits?

The media really would be rough on her because of the age

difference. . . . And who wouldn't rather be rich than not?

Come on, dummy.

He peeled the plastic from a cassette, put it in, started taping—as she came to the doorway of the bathroom, holding closed her short satin robe. She stood looking at him, a hand at the switch. The light faded low.

And came back up a little as she stood looking at him. Smiling? She went to the foam-filled tub; turned the water off. Moved to the sink, began pinning up her back hair, the robe opening to the mirror.

He checked the 3B monitors, and 3A. Crazy Susan was in the living room, eating from a lap tray, watching the tube.

He scanned the blue-white rows. Nothing major.

Watched her drop the robe at her back, raise a leg, put a foot into the foam.

He watched. . . .

Checked his watch and the clock—7:50. Turned, went to the foyer. Peeped, opened the door, went out; drew the door closed.

He opened the stairway door, went onto the landing with its black 13 and white fluorescence.

Stood with a hand on the rail, looking up through the cleft between the undersides of stairs.

She was trying to con him. No question about it.

He hurried down the zigzagging half-flights, down the gray concrete well.

HE OPENED ALL three pairs of accordion doors; went to the other side of the room and stood surveying the sparsely hung closets—shoes and suitcases on the floor, top shelves lined with boxes and bags, stacks of paperbacks.

"*I've got one in the closet myself*," Sam had said, dealing cards around the table a few weeks after he moved in. "*A jealous husband*

s
l
i
v
e
r

put out a contract on me once. Really, no shit. A jealous widower; she was dead. An actress I'd been boffing for ages. But I'm still in favor of banning them."

He remembered it somehow.

He found it on the second try, in a zippered overnight bag, wrapped in a white motel towel smelling of oil—a blue-steel automatic, *Beretta U.S.A.* on the side, the milled grip empty. Two clips of bullets in the bag, one full, one with two spaces at the bottom.

He hefted the gun in his plastic-gloved hand. Another bequest from the old man, in a way. He tucked it into the waist of his jeans, pulled the sweater down over it, patted it. Put the full clip of bullets in his left side pocket.

He zipped the bag closed with the towel and the other clip in it, put it back on the closet shelf; he would unzip it when he came down afterward to put the note by the typewriter.

He closed the accordion doors, leaving the one nearest the foyer partly open as he had found it.

Sitting at the table in the living room, he checked his watch—7:57—and studied Sam's typing, the last pages of it in the thick folder. The typing, not the words. *Thea* lay among the words. Afterward he would take those pages with him; no one would miss them.

Some of the letters were darker than the others, hit harder—B's, N's, and H's mostly. A few had been X'ed over.

He got out the draft of the note. Rolled a sheet of Sam's typing paper into the old Remington.

Jabbed Sam-style with plastic-gloved fingers at the round black keys.

The fourth try looked good:

> To Whom It May Concern,
>
> Kay Norris made ceratain promises to me which she has decided not to keep. I am going to give her one more chance to give up her young stud. If you are reaxding this, it means she refused. I made a promise to her. I keep my promises. —S.Y.

He brought it to the bookshelves, crouched, drew out one of
the large books stacked flat on the bottom shelf—*Classics of the*
Silent Screen; he put the sheet of paper inside it, on a picture of
Pauline or whoever tied to the railroad tracks; put the book in its
place in the stack.

He brushed his hands, checked the watch—8:06. Sixteen
minutes since he'd left. No sweat. She'd be half an hour at
least—Segovia, the bubbles . . .

He folded the draft of the note and the first three tries, put
them in his pocket. Swung the hinged cover down over the
typewriter, put the dictionary on the folder, the lamp and the
chair the way they had been, switched the lamp off.

He stood in the foyer doorway with a hand on the switch and
a hand on the sweater-covered gun at his waist, taking a last look
at the room—its thrift-shop furnishings no better-looking live
than on the tube.

He switched the light off, moved to the door, peeped out.

Waited while a man waited outside the door of 3A.

Waited while the door opened and Susan counted out bills,
said something, closed the door.

Waited while the man waited for the elevator.

Hurried down the stairs taking the gloves off—8:11.

He pressed the elevator button in the basement and went into
the laundry room. Denise and Allan turned from one of the
washers. He nodded to them, went to the machines.

Denise and Allan? God, he was out of touch. They moved
apart as he fed coins into slots. He bought potato chips and
catnip; hurried out to the opening number-two elevator.

Rode to thirteen.

Unlocked the door.

She was in the tub under islands of foam, her head on the rim
by the wall, her eyes closed.

He lowered himself into the chair, watching. Took out the
gun, put it on the console.

Sat watching.

Felice jumped up on the console. She sniffed the gun. Stepped over it, sniffed the X-acto knife. Pawed it; it rolled away. He picked it up. "Thanks," he said.

He put the bag of chips down and cut open the catnip's plastic shell; took out the thumb-size sack, held it toward Felice. She leaned, sniffed it. He tossed it away over his shoulder, she leaped from the console.

He turned the brightness up a little.

Watched, putting the knife in a drawer.

Sat back, watching; fished with a foot under the console, hooked out the pig.

"IT'S ME," he said.

She picked up the phone and tucked it against her shoulder, sitting cross-legged on the bed in pale pajamas. She scooped inside the container, brought out a spoonful of dark ice cream. Held it toward him, smiling.

Beep.

"No, thanks," he said. "I've got a vodka and tonic." He shook the glass so the ice tinkled; sipped from it.

She ate the spoonful of ice cream, looking at him. Asked, "Are we celebrating?"

"I don't know," he said, watching her. "I need more time to think. I'll tell you in the morning."

She scooped in the container. "Seems foolish to waste a good night. . . ." She looked at him. Ate ice cream.

He smiled and said, "I don't consider it wasted. We'll talk in the morning."

She looked at him. "I love you, baby," she said. "Don't do anything foolish."

"Don't you," he said.

■   ■   ■

IN THE MORNING he said he needed more time.

"I don't see why."

"Because I still think maybe you're conning me, that's why."

"I'm not," she said, lying on her back, looking at the light, fingering the phone wire between her breasts.

"Then *you* trust *me*. Just till this evening. I'll bring Felice up then, I promise you, safe and sound. I have to speak to my lawyer about certain things and I'm having a hard time running him down. He's in Vail, Colorado."

She said, "I want to go do some shopping."

"You can do it tomorrow. It's snowing anyway, heavily. Nobody's going out."

"I want to call Roxie, Wendy . . ."

"Just watch what you say."

"I don't want you listening!"

"Then wait till tomorrow!"

She hung up, sat up. Made a face at the light, stuck her tongue out.

She got up and went to the window, tugged with both hands at the drapery cord.

Stood with her arms folded, looking at whirling white flakes, white park, a white-quilted pinnacled roof, white gardens.

The barren windowsill, only the telescope on it.

"HELLO, MR. YALE," he said. "My name is Pete Henderson. I'm a friend of Kay Norris's, we're coming to your party next Friday. . . ."

"Oh sure," Sam said on 1, standing by the living-room table, the phone at his cheek. "We've talked in the elevator."

"That's right, I'm in thirteen A," he said. "I'll tell you why I'm calling. I just found out last night that today is Kay's birthday."

"Oh?"

"Her friend Roxie and I are setting up a little surprise party for her." He watched her vacuuming in the bedroom on 2. "At nine o'clock tonight," he said. "Her place. Kay's, I mean. Just a dozen or so people. I know she'll be pleased if you're there. . . ."

"I'd love to be," Sam said. "Thank you."

"It's apartment twenty B," he said. "And would you please make it as close to nine as possible? The logistics are kind of complicated."

"Nine on the button," Sam said.

"Thanks," he said. "See you then."

"Thank *you*," Sam said. "It'll be nice to talk about something besides the weather."

"You're right," he said, smiling. "Twenty B, nine o'clock."

They hung up.

He drew a breath.

Caressed Felice sleeping in his lap.

Watched Sam picking up the phone.

THE BEEP SOUNDED. "Hi, Jerry, it's Sam," he said. "I'm not going to be able to make it after all. I hope it doesn't screw things up; maybe Milt can sit in. Take care." He hung up.

Went over to the window.

Stood watching a snowplow clanking up the avenue sweeping a rampart of snow against the cars parked on the other side. Nice for the drivers when they got back.

He tried to think of a present he could get her, something that, while not too expensive or personal, would show wit and discernment far outshining anything young Pete Henderson had in that department.

Why did that name ring a bell?

Of course . . . Henderson had been Thea's husband's name. And hadn't her son's name been Peter? Yes . . .

Common enough, Peter Henderson . . .

This one looked to be about the right age. Had the right
coloring too—John Henderson's reddish-brown hair and blue
eyes . . .

What a coincidence *that* would be, Thea's son . . . Going,
naturally, with women who looked like her, Kay very much,
Naomi Singer a little . . .

Could it be? And did Kay know? Was Pete Henderson the one
who had told her about the bathing suits and summer dresses?

He would ask her, once the surprise part of the party was
over.

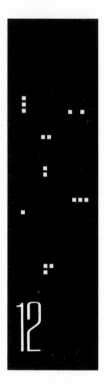

12

She stood by the coffee table, looked up at the light. "Enough is enough," she said to her upside-down self in sneakers and jeans and the burgundy turtleneck. "It's eight-fucking-thirty. I've got cabin fever. Let's go out and get burgers or something. Don't bother calling, just get your—" She turned as the hall door unlocked, opened. He came in with Felice looking around and meowing in his arm. "Hi," he said. Dumped Felice to the foyer floor.

She closed her eyes, drew breath.

Opened her eyes as Felice went to the kitchen.

"Hey, stupid, wait up," she said, going after her. Felice stopped and turned, looked at her. She crouched, picked her up, stood cradling her on her shoulder; nuzzled the calico fur, kissed it. Felice squirmed.

She carried her into the kitchen, crouched, let her jump off. "When did you feed her last?" she asked, switching the light on.

"There was stuff out."

"What, an egg roll?" She opened the cabinet, got out a can. Felice meowed at her. "Patience," she said, getting the opener from the drawer. Glanced at him as he came to the doorway. "Hi," she said.

"Hi." He smiled and looked around, his hands in his jeans pockets, a bulky greenish-tweed jacket buttoned at his waist over a light blue shirt. "It looks like *my* kitchen," he said.

Dirty dishes lay in the sink, utensils and boxes on the counters, a dish towel over the knife rack.

"Believe it or not," she said, working the can opener, "I haven't been up to my personal best the past thirty hours or so. That's nice tweed."

"Ancient," he said.

"Did you speak to your lawyer?" She crouched, spooning food into the bowl while Felice stood watching.

She glanced up at him. He shook his head.

She spooned the food. "What have you decided?" she asked.

"Let's talk about it inside," he said.

She put the can in the garbage, the spoon in the sink. "How about over burgers at Jackson Hole?" she said. "I've got cabin fever."

He said, "Let's talk first, okay?"

She rinsed the water bowl and filled it, put it down.

Went to him, smiled, kissed his lips. "Want a drink?" she asked.

He shook his head. Kissed her lips.

They went into the living room, hooking fingers on the way. Parted at the sofa, went around it. She sat; he went to the window.

He split the white silk panels with a finger, looked out between them. "It's starting again," he said.

"I'd still like to go out," she said. Sat watching him, sitting against the sofa's right arm, a folded leg on the cushion, a hand on her denimed knee.

He went toward the other end of the sofa; stopped beside the coffee table, stood looking at her. Breathed a sigh. "Honey," he said, "I would give anything if I could believe you. I mean it. But I just can't see you forgetting about *murders*, especially when one of them was someone you knew, even if it was only slightly."

She said, looking at him, "You're underestimating how much you mean to me, and how appalled I am when I think about the publicity. I'm not saying I'm going to be blissfully happy, that I won't be bothered sometimes." She shrugged. "It's the best choice there is," she said. "From my selfish viewpoint, and from yours too, I would think. Unless you don't want to marry someone my age no matter what."

"Oh, come on," he said. He backed to the side chair and sat on the edge of it, shook his head. "No," he said, "you were afraid I'd jump, and you wanted Felice back." Felice crossed the rug before him, black-tipped tail swaying. "Good girl, right on cue," he said. "I've been training her."

They watched as Felice sank down on the cushion beneath the window, licked a paw, pawed her face. "I really enjoyed having her," he said.

They looked at each other.

She said, "What can I do to convince you I mean it?"

"You can't," he said. Unbuttoned his jacket, folded his hands between his knees, sat looking at her.

She said, "Are you going to turn yourself in?"

"And spend my life in a loony bin? If I'm lucky?"

"It wouldn't be your life," she said.

"Watching network TV in the day room . . ." He smiled. "Arguing with the other loons about which channel. No. . . ." He shook his head and bent it, rubbed at the reddish-brown hair.

She sat with her hand on her knee, watching him. "You know,
Pete," she said, "that if—anything were to happen to me, even if
it looked like an accident or suicide, or a break-in or whatever—
now, so soon after Sheer died . . ."

"I know," he said. "I'd be the number-one suspect."

She leaned toward him. "Baby, listen to me," she said. "With
a good lawyer you could be out in a lot less time than you think,
and you can afford the best, can't you? There's the good that
you've done, the money you sent to people, that'll be considered
too. And again, the fact that you turned yourself in, that would
be *bound* to be a big point in your favor, I know it would.
Honestly, baby."

He raised his head, looked at her.

She said, "It won't be so terrible. . . ." Smiled at him. "You'll
get love letters from women of all ages."

He said, "Sam is coming up."

She looked at him.

He reached inside his jacket. "This is his," he said. "My father
put out a contract on him after *my mother* died. That's when he
got it. It's a Beretta, nine millimeter."

She looked at the blue-steel gun in his hand.

"It's going to be a murder-suicide," he said. "He's been
making annoying phone calls. Nothing major, I don't think you
even mentioned them to anyone except me." He rested his wrist
on his thigh, the gun in his hand tipped downward. "He
misinterpreted some things you said in the park a while back.
He was after you to stop seeing me—you know how jealous old
men can get. They're going to find a note about it next to his
typewriter. I typed it last night while you were in the tub." He
smiled. "Not the whole time, the first twenty-five minutes or
so."

She said, "Why is he coming?"

"For a surprise party," he said. "It's your birthday." He
glanced at his watch, put his hand to the gun between his knees,
fingers stroking the barrel. "The funny thing is," he said, "he's
the one I really wanted to get all along. That's why I brought

him here, I was going to watch him and then do it when I found a safe way. Thea—*my mother* was going to *him*, to stay with him, when . . . They had a fight about it before the party, she and my father. She didn't fall down the stairs, he pushed her, I saw." He drew a breath. "It was Sam's fault as much as his," he said. "But then I—had to deal with Billy Webber. And Brendan Connahay died right after. So he got a new lease on life, Sam. On his apartment too." He smiled. "He turned out to be pretty interesting, with the acting lessons, the for-real ones *and* the others. I won't tell you what the proportion was." He raised the gun, slid back its top and released it, aimed it at her, his finger on the trigger. "Do you have a knife under the cushion?" he asked.

She sat looking at him.

"Pretty cool," he said. "I didn't see you getting it there. Take it out now. Slowly, just with two fingers, not so you could throw it at me, and put it on the coffee table. Right now."

She put her hand down in behind the cushion and brought out—thumb and forefinger lifting the black handle—a wide-heeled twelve-inch knife with a pointed tip. She passed it to the thumb and forefinger of her other hand, reached, lowered it onto the coffee table.

She sat straight, folded her arms. Sat looking at him aiming the gun at her.

He lowered it. "It's you or me, Kay," he said. Glanced at his watch.

"When's the party?" she asked.

"At nine," he said.

"What if he doesn't come?"

"He will," he said. "He dropped out of a string quartet he plays in and he got you a present. When I left he was pressing his pants."

"Why did you have to 'deal' with Billy Webber?" she asked.

"He found out the phones were bugged," he said. "He was blackmailing me."

"How did he find out?" she asked. Unfolded her arms.

He smiled. "He dealt drugs, he was paranoid about security," he said. "He brought home a high-tech bug detector one night and got a positive signal. I almost fell through the floor. It was only a few weeks after people started moving in and I was still kind of nervous and excited about everything."

"What did you do?" she asked.

"I ran right down there," he said. "He was in six A. I told him I was the owner and I'd gotten a signal he used a detector. I said I'd bugged the phones for kicks. We made a deal." His hands held the gun between his knees, the muzzle down. "I gave him, I think it was two thousand dollars the first time," he said. "I kept quiet about the drugs and he kept quiet about the bugging. Then he wanted more money, and more—*much* more, exactly the way blackmailers are supposed to. So I went in one day and switched some of his stuff around. It was such an easy thing to do. . . ." He sighed, glanced at his watch. Smiled at her. "Rafael, the super, was a funny situation," he said. "It could have been a sitcom. *The Odd Couple.* He got curious about thirteen B and picked the lock one day when I was out. He didn't know I was involved, he just didn't want me around to see him doing it. When I got back, there he was at the console."

"More blackmail?" she said.

"A little," he said. "A couple of hundred a week. The problem was he got into watching, like you. He was in there four or five hours a day and at least two nights a week, running everything himself most of the time, neglecting his duties—and there was nothing I could do about it. Then he wanted to bring his wife. Next it would've been the kids. . . ." He sighed, shrugged. "She got a big cash settlement, Mrs. Ortiz," he said.

"I know," she said, watching him, sitting with her hands on her knees.

He said, "What did you do, look things up?"

She nodded.

He nodded. "Sure," he said.

"Did Naomi get hooked too?" she asked.

He shook his head. Looked at her. "She wouldn't let me turn

it on," he said. "She was your standard knee-jerk liberal, practically in tears about the civil-rights violation. I didn't tell her, she figured things out herself. Channel Thirteen had run a *Nova* on electronic surveillance, and I made some dumb mistakes"—he glanced at his watch—"little things like knowing where she kept the place mats. Yes, we had an affair, but we only got together every week or so. She was uptight about it." He smiled. "On account of our age difference—seven years. I was twenty-four then, she was thirty-one."

She said, "She was going to tell?"

He nodded.

"You made her write the letter. . . ."

"No, *I* wrote it," he said, smiling. "I pasted it together out of lines from one of her notebooks and then I made copies of it, good and dark, on a machine. Then I traced it about fifty times, till I was writing it, you know, with a flow. I had plenty of time; I gave a hundred thousand dollars to Greenpeace and she gave me a month to get the monitors out." He glanced at his watch.

She said, "I suppose in the beginning you—" He stood up, pointing the gun at her. "We have to go inside now," he said. "If you scream you'll be wasting your breath, Vida is out and so is Phil." He stamped on the rug. "And the Ostrows are really having a party. That's why I made it this late."

She sat looking at him. "Please, baby . . ." she said.

He leaned at her. "There's no other *way*," he said. "Believe me, I was up all *night* trying to think of one. You're like Rocky. Sheer. Even if you *swore* you would take a bribe I wouldn't believe you. Come on. Now." He poked upward with the gun.

She drew breath, shifted around, got up catching and slinging the knife at his head; lunged at him over the corner of the table as he ducked. They hit the arm of the chair; it fell sideward, spilling them to the rug; Felice meowed and ran.

They rolled, she on top grabbing at the wrist of his gun hand. His other hand caught her throat, pushed her back; she clutched his arm as he rolled over her. He let go and got up, holding the gun; stood panting as she climbed to her knees holding on to the coffee table, rubbing her throat.

"I can do it in here too," he said. "I'm flexible." She flung the Magritte book in his groin, grabbed his wrist with both hands as he bent, twisted his arm around over her shoulder, turning and hipping up under him. He howled, punching her other shoulder; she pulled the gun from his fingers, ducked and turned, backed toward the window, taking the gun in both hands, aiming it at him as he crouched holding his shoulder, rubbing his arm, blue eyes staring at her. Felice meowed, standing in the pass-through.

They panted, watching each other.

"I fired a gun like this at a range in Syracuse," she said. "Get over by the wall there."

Watching her, he took a step to the side. "Kay . . ." he said.

"Go on," she said, holding the gun with both hands, her finger on the trigger. "Don't say anything. I don't want to hear one more word out of you."

He stood still. "How about good-bye?" he said. Turned and ran.

She followed him with the gunsight, didn't squeeze, watched him run—not to the hall but through the foyer into the bedroom, slamming the door.

She lowered the gun.

Stared at the closed door.

Ran to it.

Stopped—cold circling her ankles.

A snowflake blew from under the door, became a speck of wet on the wood.

She closed her eyes, drew breath.

Pushed the door against wind. Opened it to the wall.

The draperies billowed and flapped in the lamplit bedroom, the left side of the window open to wind and snowflakes and darkness.

She stood staring. Swallowed.

Leaned against the door jamb, shut her eyes, the gun at her side.

Drew breath.

Sighed it out. Went in, put the gun on the bed. Stood hugging her sweatered arms, her eyes tearing.

She knuckled at the corners of them, went to the window. Pushed billowing drapery aside, spread her arms and grasped cold bronze framing with both hands. Leaned into the wind and snowflakes, looked down at white far below. The wind dropped, accordion doors rolled. She spun around, he came pushing at her middle; pushed her backward out the window.

13

Cloth brushed her hand, she clutched, it pulled her; she grabbed with her other hand, swinging around; hung from handfuls of chintz and muslin, kicking air. Her shoulder hit brick, her sneakered foot slid against glass. She stared up at him staring out the window at her. The drapery quivered; she stared up at its top inside the window.

An end hook popped from the muslin header, the next hook popped, the next, the row of hooks popping as, hitching herself upward, she caught the window track with one hand and the other; pulled, hauling her knees up to the bricks; pushed with her knees and thighs, pulled with her arms and fingers. Wind hit her back, the drapery flapped into the window, the door inside slammed.

"Shit," he said, shaking his head, grimacing down at her. "*Shit . . .*"

She hung from the outer metal track, staring up at him.

"I *can't!*" he cried. "I've got to think of *me!*" He went from the window.

Staring at dark wet bricks, her knees mashed against a dent of mortar, arms and fingers aching, she squirmed her left hand's fingers toward the window panel a few inches away. If she could get a decent grip where it met the track, climb up the bricks . . . And not think about hanging twenty stories high in wind and snow from the back of a sliver building . . . An icy trickle slithered down her spine; she shivered. Hung by arms and fingers, pushed with thighs and knees, squirmed fingers leftward in the cold wet metal track, not looking down. Just another invigorating workout. At the Vertical Club . . .

"It's *still* going to work."

She looked up at him.

He sat sideways on the sill, squinting against snowflakes, his hands shiny in plastic, wiping the gun. "*He's* the one you fought with," he said, "then he chased you in here, pushed you out, shot himself. He'll be here in four minutes and I pray to God he isn't late." He tucked the gun inside his jacket, squinted into the wind, frowning. "Maybe I ought to push *him*. . . ."

She hooked her fingers in behind the panel, pulled with both aching arms; worked her right knee—getting numb, the denim wet through—up to the next dent in the bricks; worked her left knee up. Pushed with both knees, crept her right hand's fingers into the inner track.

He stood up and picked up the telescope, grasped its narrow end in his plastic-gloved hand. Crouched and hooked the wide end's edge under her two middle fingertips in the track. Lifted at them. "*I'm never going to forget you,*" he called against the wind. "*I've got the tapes. Last night, and the night you moved in—*

that's pretty poor quality though—and that Saturday night . . . Six weeks ago, almost to the minute . . ." He smiled, crouching, lifting at her fingertips with the telescope—gently, so as not to mark them. "*We've certainly run the gamut, haven't we?*" he called. "*God, I wish it didn't have to end this way. I'm going to watch you as long as I live.* Scoot, Felice."

Felice came walking along the windowsill.

"Scoot," he said.

Felice stopped, looked at him—and walked on, to the fingers hooked down around the corner of the outer panel. Sniffed them.

She recoiled, hissing, her fur ruffling.

He stood up. "Scram," he said. "Mommy's busy falling."

Felice leaned, sniffed the tight-pressed fingers, hissed at them. She took another step, put her head out around the panel, shied at the wind and snowflakes. Looked down at the face staring up at her.

Drew back, sniffed the fingers.

Turned, hissing. Reared back along the sill.

"Cool it," he said. "It's me. Daddy."

She snarled up at him, eyes narrowed; hissed, showed her teeth, wriggled her haunches, tail straight back.

"Fuck off, Felice," he said. Poked the telescope at her. "Or would you rather—" She shot hissing from his arm to his face, caught his nose in her teeth, dug her claws through his eyelids. The telescope flew as he clutched her, shiny hands sliding. He screamed in her fur, falling backward.

NARY A SOUL in the twentieth-floor hallway. He checked his watch as the elevator door slid closed behind him: nine on the button, the hands at a perfect ninety-degree angle.

He wondered what exactly were Pete Henderson's complicated logistics. Checked himself in the mirror—red-eyed, rotten-looking. Fixed the collar of the jacket so the frayed place was hidden—for the moment.

He moved to the 20B door. Listened. No sound of people. He pressed the button; the bell ding-donged.

He studied the beribboned little box from Dollhouse Antics. Hoped he hadn't gotten too cute. Too late now . . .

A cry from inside?

He tried the doorknob; it turned.

He opened the door a few inches. Lights were on. "*Hello?*" he called toward the living room. "*Anybody home?*"

A gargled moan from the bedroom.

He opened the door wider. The kitchen looked messy; he'd figured her for neat. A soaring bird, a knockout painting of a falcon or a hawk or something, hung between the kitchen and the bathroom. The bedroom door was closed.

"*Hello?*" he called, going in. He put the box on a Victorian coat rack, steadied the wobbly marble shelf. Jumped aside as a knife fell from under it.

He looked at it lying on the floor—a pointed kitchen knife seven or eight inches long, with a black handle.

He picked it up, looked at it. Put it on the shelf with the box.

Went to the bedroom door. Coldness blew from under it. He knocked. "*Kay?*" he called. "*It's Sam Yale. Are you all right?*"

A moan.

He pushed the door against wind. A cat raced out—orange, red, white—raced for the living room, black-tipped tail fluffed.

He opened the door wider. Stared, his heart sinking.

A blood-faced man sat on the floor against the side of the bed by its foot, moaning, holding cupped blood-lumped hands toward him. Pete Henderson. With red-black hollows for eyes— like an actor made up for Oedipus's final entrance. A path of torn-down twisted drapery ran to the open window where— Christ!—*someone climbing in* lifted a dark head, looked at him— He rushed past Henderson, got down on a knee by her, his heart pounding. Grabbed the back of her belt, got an arm beneath her—she was cold, shivering, in a wet dark turtleneck—helped lift her up onto the sill. She brought her legs up, rolling onto her side, wincing, the frayed knees of her jeans bloodied. "My *God!*" he said. A moan from Henderson.

He helped her sit up and swing her legs down; pulled the window closed behind her, stood, closed it all the way. Unbuttoned his jacket. "*I'll call an ambulance in a second!*" he shouted.

"I can hear," Henderson said.

She sat panting on the sill, shivering, staring toward Henderson, her arms folded tight, hands tucked in armpits. Her hair was tangled, wet, her lips bluish. She turned to him as he put his jacket around her shoulders. "Felice?" she said. "My cat?"

"It ran into the living room," he said.

She unfolded her arms, pushed against the sill. "The shower," she said.

He helped her stand. "What in God's *name?*" he asked. He walked with her on the drapery, steadying her; watched her panting, shivering. Henderson moaned. She kept close to the closets, looking ahead. He held her at the waist and shoulder of his jacket.

She said, "He was—going to—kill us both. . . ."

"*Why?*" he asked.

"He killed the others," she said. "The building is bugged. With videocameras."

"*What?*"

She took his jacket off at the door. "He owns it," she said. "There's the phone. Watch out, he has your gun." She gave him the jacket, looked at him. "He's Thea Marshall's son," she said.

"I *thought* he might be! *Videocameras?* Go, go, I'm sorry."

She went into the bathroom, switching the light on. Closed the door and locked it.

Toed her sneakers off. Went into the shower.

Grasped the chrome Art Deco handle. Turned the water hot.

She stripped in the downpour, examined her raw knees, her hands and fingers, massaged her arms.

Turned the water hotter.

Stood hugging herself, weeping.

· · ·

WHEN THEY GOT out of the patrol car in front of Horror High-Rise, at a little after two by Sam's watch, halogen lights glared on tripods at both sides of the canopy, vans were double-parked, another van came skidding around the corner from Ninety-second Street. Black cameras swooped at them, riding men's shoulders; Sam warded them off right and left with his raised finger; Walt brandished a snow shovel.

They made it into the lobby, where twenty or more of the tenants were huddled around radios and agreements to join in class-action lawsuits.

"Is the building really *bugged*?" Vida asked. "Yes," she said. Dmitri said, "He killed Rafael, *everybody*?" "Not Brendan Connahay," she said. "They took out tapes," Stefan said. "Were those of us?" She nodded. "Is he blind?" someone asked.

"Yes," Sam said. "Folks," he said, standing with his hands raised and his back to the elevators, "we spoke to reporters at the police station; you can read about it in the papers tomorrow. I don't want to be unneighborly but we've had a rough night, especially Ms. Norris. Peter Henderson is in Metropolitan Hospital under police guard. He isn't watching *anything* any more. If you have questions, the man to speak to is Detective Wright at the Nineteenth Precinct. You'll find him very pleasant and courteous. Thank you."

They rode up in the right-hand elevator.

SHE MADE REAL coffee. They drank it on the sofa, Felice curled sleeping in her lap.

He said, "That's going to be the most famous cat in the country. She's going to get a date with Morris from Nine Lives."

She sipped from her mug. "A lot of good it'll do them both," she said.

He smiled, watching her. Sipped, looked at the ceiling light. "Incredible," he said. "TV madness . . . I guess it was inevitable that someone would come down with it sooner or later."

"He's not the first case," she said. "There's a hotel that's bugged too, and a couple of other apartment houses. At least that's what he said. Sam, listen." She looked at him. "I want you to know, I never watched *you*. It was a condition at the outset: not you, not the bathrooms."

"Nice you were fastidious," he said.

"You have no idea how hypnotic it is," she said. "It's impossible to stop watching. There's always something going on and even the prosaic things become interesting, because it's real and you never know what's going to happen next."

They sipped from their mugs.

She said, "I'm going down there. There are tapes I don't think they found that I want to get rid of, tapes of me; and the ones they're looking for could be there too, though he may have erased them. But I have a feeling he didn't, not if he was taping tonight."

"You lost me," he said.

"Never mind," she said. "The point is I'm going down to thirteen B, do you want to come?"

They looked at each other.

"I mean just to look," she said. "Not to watch."

He said, "Won't it be sealed?"

"With a strip of tape, I suppose," she said. "I have a key. Don't worry, I'm going to tell Detective Wright exactly what I did and why I did it, even if I don't find the other tapes. I'm sure he'll understand. If he doesn't, it'll be my responsibility."

He scratched his ear. "Well . . ." he said, "I guess I ought to. Just on the off chance I wind up directing the miniseries."

"What do you mean, 'the off chance'?" she said, leaning and putting her mug down. "We'll make it part of the deal." She gathered Felice in her arms, got up and turned; winced, raising a foot. "Ooh Jesus, my knees," she said.

"Ahhh," he said, wincing, watching her as he got up.

She put Felice down in the hollow in the cushion. Bent, kissed her head. "Good cat," she said. "What a cat." Kissed her nose. "Tuna steak from here on in."

Felice hunkered down in the apricot velvet, purring, eyes closed. Her whiskers twitched.

They headed for the foyer. She said, "I'll bet everybody in the building is still up talking about everything."

He opened the hall door, held it for her. "I wouldn't mind taking one little peek," he said, going out after her.

IRA LEVIN's earlier novels are *A Kiss Before Dying*, *Rosemary's Baby*, *This Perfect Day*, *The Stepford Wives*, and *The Boys from Brazil*. His plays include *No Time for Sergeants*, *Cantorial*, and the longest-running thriller in Broadway history, *Deathtrap*.

Born in New York City in 1929 and an alumnus of New York University, he began his career in television's "golden age," writing plays for *Lights Out* and *The United States Steel Hour*. He has won two Edgar Allan Poe Awards, serves on the council of the Dramatists Guild, and lives in the Carnegie Hill district of Manhattan in which *Sliver* is set. He has three sons.